THE COMMON THREAD

CC SMITH
BETTY GORDON

L & L Dreamspell
London, Texas

Cover and Interior Design by L & L Dreamspell

ISBN: 978-1-60318-310-9

Library of Congress Control Number: 2011921572

Visit us on the web at www.lldreamspell.com

Published by L & L Dreamspell
Printed in the United States of America

For Rhonda, my dear daughter-in-law,
who lost her battle with cancer in 2010.
and
For Tom, my husband, who showers me
with love and support.

⁓ Betty

Dedicated with love to
Lee, Kim, Zoey, and Zack

And for my Knight, Harry

⁓CC

There are a thousand hacking at the branches of evil
to one who is striking at the root.
Henry David Thoreau

I couldn't get the woman's voice out of my mind.
It was hypnotic. Her message shattered life as
we know it.
   M. Adams
   2007

ONE

Michael Adams walked out his back door into a yard beautifully illuminated by a full moon. He looked at the silver blue ring encircling it, ice crystals promised winter. He savored the quiet moment. Suddenly, a strong gust of wind grabbed and swirled the remaining autumn leaves at his feet, creating ominous whispers through the pines—murmurs that sent shivers down his back. He scanned the area. Over the last month, he'd been unable to shake this strange, uneasy feeling. This sensation wasn't new—always an omen for the unexpected. Dark clouds closed in on the moon forming eerie shadows on the lawn wrapping him in darkness. Michael took a deep breath and asked for protection. Traces of moonlight played on the turrets of his house—a forewarning?

The slamming of his neighbor's door jerked him out of his trance. He hurried toward his car—time to get to work.

Traffic was heavy for this time of night, probably a game in town. He flipped radio stations hoping to hear something other than dire news. He shook his head. Not much good happening in the world.

His evening talk show at EPOH radio was one of the joys of his life. He couldn't wait to sink his teeth into tonight's broadcast. A recent judicial ruling lit *his* fire and he wanted to fan the flames with the public. It was bizarre any rational human being could award probation to a child-molester. Something was definitely wrong and something needed to be done. He hoped the debate on this evening's program would turn up some answers.

As he drove, his sister's image played in his head. As always, sadness followed remembrances of Celeste. He pounded the steering wheel with his fist. *What a lousy big brother. Big brothers are supposed to take care of their little sisters. It's been twenty-eight years. Where are you, Celeste? How young and stupid I was back then. I hope I'm wiser now and, God knows, I'm certainly older.*

Children need protection. They need a champion. That's what my show is about.

Hell, that's what my life is about. If I wanted to play it safe, I would have gotten into a different line of work.

He had little time to catch his breath before taking his seat and greeting his guests, retired judges and lawyers. He had to keep his cool—there was a lot riding on tonight. He was on.

Michael started the child-molestation debate with some hard-hitting questions about laws protecting children. Accusations and criticisms soared around the table. Accountability and solutions grew into pompous rhetoric. The call board blazed with lights, but he waited for the dialog to heat up. When he smelled smoke, he answered calls.

"Hello, Chicago."

"Hey, Michael. Love your show. I can't believe this could happen. What kind of man is this Judge Evans? Obviously, he doesn't have kids."

"I agree, man. Thanks for calling."

"New York?"

"Michael, I think the judges who let the guys or gals walk are sick. Makes me wonder why they empathize with these criminals. Are they cut from the same cloth?"

"Whoa! I don't think we want to go down that path—that's another show. Thanks for your call."

"Arkansas, you're on."

"Michael, Reverend Shaw here. I really enjoy your show. I

didn't agree with what Judge Evans did, but I do think some of these troubled people who harm children can be saved and should be given a chance. 'Vengeance is mine, says the Lord.' I preach forgiveness every Sunday to my congregation."

"Sorry, Reverend, but I couldn't disagree with you more. I think we have enough data on child molesters to know very few change. They might want to, doctors prescribe drugs hoping they will, but sometimes hideous beasts lie just beneath the surface waiting for reasons to strike."

"Alabama, let's hear from you."

"God forgive me, but until you experience the pain—" he hesitated— "you have no idea. I say Reverend Shaw is wrong. I think we should take revenge here on earth, let God handle them when they're dead. I say kill the bastards."

"I understand. Ohio, what's on your mind?"

"Well, Michael, I'm shocked the gentleman from New York would come up with such a ridiculous idea about our judges. I'm sure all our judges are fine, upstanding people. Cut from the same cloth—what a terrible thing to imply."

"I'm sure most of our judges *are* fine people."

"California, you're on."

"I see no excuse to ever take a life."

"Well, that's debatable."

Michael started wrapping up the night's session by reviewing listeners' outrage that a judge would give a child-molester probation. Most callers demanded Judge Evans step down, others agreed that molesters deserved a second chance, some suggested counseling.

The director motioned to Michael—lines were closing.

"Thanks to all for sharing your opinions. We'll be back tomorrow night with—"

"Michael?" A woman's captivating voice drifted through the studio.

Michael looked toward the director in the control booth. Bob raised both hands showing he had nothing to do with the caller.

"Michael," the voice continued, "time is of the essence. I'm very troubled. My world is filled with evil that's spreading like fungus on a tree, and the tree is dying. It seemed insignificant when it started, but now it's consuming the whole tree. My question is, should I let it die a slow painful death or end it now?"

"Wait, please. End what? Let's talk about this. Things can't be all that bad."

Bob's voice played in his ear. "Keep her talking—we have some time to kill."

When the caller didn't get a response, she began again. "Michael, are you still there? I need someone to tell me what to do. I hope you and your listeners can give me some advice on how to get the evil out of my world."

Michael ran his fingers through his hair and tried to sound composed. "Exactly what evil are you talking about?"

"You discuss it every day on your show—people who destroy children, kill, steal, start wars in the name of their gods. Right now, Michael, there is more hate than love in my world, more evil than good. It's not the first time this has happened. I've handled it in the past, or thought I had. Some good died with the bad, but this time I let it go on too long. Now it's widespread." She hesitated and a heartfelt sigh drifted through the studio.

"You know, I would love to help you. I don't want anybody to die. Unfortunately, my air time is over, but I'd like to stay and talk with you off air."

"Oh, Michael, maybe my timing is wrong. I'll say goodbye for now. I'll try to sort this out."

"Well, folks, sorry we have to end without a response for our intriguing caller, but regrettably I must say good night."

As he went off air, he stared at Bob. "What the hell was that about? You kept me on the hot seat way too long. Christ, look at my shirt, it's soaked. Why did you keep me on air with a nut case?"

Bob tried to smile. "Calm down. Something is screwed up."

"You think?"

"Easy, man. She popped up at the last minute, I got so caught up in her voice that by the time I looked for a way to cut her off, she did it herself. I have to tell you though, I wouldn't mind if she called back—the switchboard lit up like the New York skyline. Time stood still for a few minutes. What a voice. If she's not too crazy, maybe I'll hire her."

Three weeks passed. Michael scanned the material in front of him as he listened to Alex, the news gal, wind down the hourly update. The news reminded him of his despondent caller. *If she thinks her world is in danger, how about the chaos erupting all over the globe—war escalating, horrific storms causing major flooding and deaths, earthquakes, riots in major cities—so many dying and dead.*

Her voice haunted his dreams. She sounded so young and troubled. He shook his head recalling some of the woman's words as the station manager started his countdown to resume the Hope Foundation segment.

"Welcome back, folks. I want to thank Stephen Whitney for being our guest. The Hope Foundation has spread itself so thin helping disaster victims that they need your support now more than ever. They will be thankful for any and all donations. Be sure to tune in tomorrow when my guest will be General Vincent Johnson, one of the President's staff members."

"Michael, I need to talk to you." Her voice floated around him in delicate waves.

"I'm glad to hear from you. Your last call concerned us." He looked up at the control booth to see Bob shrugging again.

"We haven't heard from you in quite some time. I'm pleased you're still with us."

"Oh, I'm *always* listening. I'm disappointed no one has come up with an answer for me yet. My world is so grim."

"Well, I think we're all worried about our future."

He hesitated listening to Bob's voice in his ear. "Keep talking. We're trying to figure out how the hell she got through. Get her name."

"We need someone to come up with an answer for all of us. By the way, you know my name, but I don't know yours. What shall I call you?"

"It doesn't matter."

"I'd like to call you by your given name."

"Pick one. I go by many names."

Michael hesitated. "Okay if I call you Celeste?"

"Celeste is a lovely name."

"Yes, I've always liked it." Michael said softly.

"I need help, Michael. I have tried everything I know to destroy the evil. It's going to be hard to get rid of all of it. I've grown to love so much and so many."

"Now wait. As I said before, there is always hope. Things can get better."

"Hope, Michael, a beautiful word. Do you think your listeners have enough to save my world?"

"I don't know if we have enough to save ourselves, but we can't give up, can we?"

"No, I don't want to give up. I'll give it more time. Thanks, Michael. Goodbye for now."

Dead air broke the spell.

The call board flashed.

Michael struggled to find his voice. "Hey, Philly, good to hear from you."

"Hello. I'm a big fan of the Hope Foundation. Thanks for having them on. I'll send a considerable contribution. I'm also glad to hear from your caller again. I'm sure all your listeners are worried about her—she sounds so distraught. If she's still listening, please seek help."

"Thanks for your encouraging words for our caller."

"California, what do you have to say?"

"Hey, man. First time caller. Enjoy your show."

"Welcome. Glad you joined us."

"Thanks, but what's with that woman caller? Is she some kind of kook?"

"I think she's just troubled."

"Yeah, we all have troubles, so how the heck does she think we're going to solve hers?"

Michael responded, "Well, there's professional help out there for everyone."

"Colorado, let's hear from you."

"I loved what your caller had to say about hope; I need a lot of it in my world too. You can count on me to follow up with a nice donation to the Foundation."

"Thanks, next caller. Jersey, you're on."

"Michael, I agree with that other guy. I think that woman who called is a major kook. Actually, I think she sounds dangerous."

"I hate to end on that note, folks, but our time is up. Thanks for listening and remember—hope *is* a beautiful word. I *hope* to see all of you back tomorrow."

Michael looked at the crew before turning toward Bob. "Jesus, this is too weird. What's going on?"

"I don't have a clue, but you can be sure we'll find out. Someone has to be tampering with our equipment and when we find out who it is, there'll be hell to pay. There's no question she's a sad woman, Michael, but damn, her voice is so engaging. The listeners love her. Our ratings soared the first time she called and the lights flashing on the board today did my old heart good."

"Damn, Bob, I don't give a rat's ass about all that. What worries me the most is she says she's always listening. What the hell does that mean?"

"You're overreacting."

Michael massaged the back of his neck. "Yeah, maybe. I don't know why, but her calls are disturbing."

Bob slapped him on the back. "Settle down, buddy. You know this business is filled with weird people, nothing we haven't seen before. I'll get to the bottom of it."

Michael was relieved when the day ended. He stopped in the men's room before heading home. As he ran wet fingers through his black hair, he studied himself in the mirror. *Not bad for a forty-five year old with a wife and three kids—more lines around my mouth than I'd like and more gray in my hair, but as long as my baby blues and strong jaw still turn my wife on, I'm good to go.*

He leaned on the basin wondering why this particular caller set him on edge. He'd had strange callers before. "Hell," he said aloud, "I've even had my life threatened—all she's doing is telling my audience about her sadness. Bob's right—I'm paranoid."

As he made his way to the parking lot and toward his Austin-Healy, he couldn't help smiling. *Good ole dad. I still can't believe he gave me his favorite toy. Time to put the day behind me and concentrate on getting home to my family.*

As he put his key in the car door, a noise made him spin around toward the stairway. "Who's there?" He saw nothing. He had to get a grip. After all, this caller was more in his head than anywhere else.

Two

The station was an easy twenty minutes from Michael's house, but it would take at least forty-five tonight. It didn't matter—it would give him a chance to clear his head. He called his wife. "Hey, baby, catch the show?"

"Of course, and I heard your lady again. I'm concerned for her."

"So am I, Rachel, but I'm sure she'll be all right. Listen, traffic's heavier than usual, so…"

"It'll take you longer—gotcha. Take care and get here in one piece."

"Will do. Love you."

He pulled in the driveway and sat in the car for a few minutes struggling again with the woman's voice playing over and over in his head. He leaned back reminding himself to forget it for now. The rest of the night belonged to family.

As soon as he stepped through the door, the warmth of the entry took away the day's worries. Restoring this old Victorian house had been a lot of work, but it was an act of love that he and Rachel enjoyed every day. He loosened his tie and threw his briefcase on the bench.

"Honey, where are you? Looks like a storm is kicking up."

"In the kitchen. Give me a minute to close the windows and I'll grab a couple of beers."

"Where are the kids?"

"They're spending the night with friends. So, my darling, we have the house to ourselves."

"I like the sound of that. I'll get a fire going in the library."

After putting a couple of fresh logs in the fireplace, he collapsed on the oversized leather couch and shut his eyes. The warmth of the fire and kitchen aromas eased his mind.

Rachel checked the pot roast, got the drinks, and slipped into the room. She stood for a moment watching the fire cast shadows on Michael's face. He looked tired and drawn. The day had taken its toll.

When Michael sensed her presence, he reached for her hand. "I've missed you today."

"Good to hear."

"Well, it's true. Come here, baby."

Rachel smiled as she laced her fingers through his. She snuggled close brushing her hand along the side of his face, playing with his hair.

"I love playing with your curls."

"You're the *only* one who can do that. I've been teased my whole life about my curls. I'm getting a haircut tomorrow, short is better."

"Fine, but curls are sexy and short is not better."

Michael laughed as he wrapped his arms around her.

"Ummm, feels good. You're way too serious, Mike. You look exhausted."

"You can say that again."

"I might also say you look worried. Is it about your lady?"

"She's not my lady—you're my lady."

"Okay, but she sounds so sad."

"I know, but we can't get personally involved. The woman obviously has problems. I don't want her problems becoming ours. You know as well as I do that sometimes people fixate on celebrities."

Rachel raised her eyebrows. "Celebrities?"

"Hell, you know what I mean. It's not about me. I'm worried about you and the kids."

"That's nonsense. This woman is lonely and needs helps. I'm

not a psychiatrist, but I don't think she's a threat."

"Let's drop it. Besides, we may not hear from her again. It's hard to think about anything other than the delicious aromas coming from the kitchen, and you." He tightened his embrace before turning off the light. Rachel's hair glowed in the firelight. "You are so lovely." He pressed his lips against hers, lightly at first before growing more intense.

Rachel trailed her fingers along his chest and sighed as they melted into the soft leather. "Feels like you're thinking about something other than dinner."

"Guess so. I'm thinking about how my curls turn you on and short is not better."

Now it was Rachel's turn to laugh.

Just then a gust of wind forced a tree limb to graze the library window as rain pelted with unrelenting force. Wind howled down the chimney causing the fire to wane.

Michael jumped up. "Sounds like the storm is coming at us with a vengeance. I better check the house."

Rachel moved toward the kitchen as he ran up the steps. When he returned, she was setting out the food.

"All quiet upstairs."

Rachel smiled. "That was a mood breaker."

"Not really, but let's toss the beers." He winked at Rachel. "My mood calls for wine. How about you?" Michael held up his glass. "Here's to my sexy wife."

"Here's to my husband that I love dearly, despite his celebrity status."

They ate in relaxed silence as the storm wailed outside.

Michael leaned back in his chair, "Hmm, since you mentioned it, it would be fun for you to play one of my adoring fans tonight." He stood and took her hand, "Come with me. I'll help you clean up in the morning."

Early sun filtered through the lace curtains. Rachel groaned looking at the clock. She turned toward Michael. There was just enough light to see him lying on his back, eyes open.

He rolled to his side. "You woke up early, Rach."

"You didn't get much sleep either, did you?" She leaned over and kissed him softly. "I'm surprised you didn't get a good night's sleep. I thought *this* fan wore you out last night."

Michael pulled her close and whispered in his sexiest voice, "Believe me, you did. I just have a lot on my mind."

Rachel bit her lower lip. "Sweetie, I know why you named the woman Celeste."

"I know you do."

"I don't know if it's wise to use your sister's name. Whenever this woman calls, it will be a constant reminder."

"I don't need a name or a phone call to remind me. The pain of losing my sister is with me every day."

"I know, but naming this woman after her only brings back the troubled past. You two had so many happy moments. None of us know what happened to Celeste, but whatever it was, it wasn't your fault."

"I'm not so sure about that. I should have been able to protect her, but all that mattered to me and my friends back then was football and cheerleaders. God, it was such a long time ago, but the memories are still as vivid as…"

"Michael, don't go there."

"Maybe I need to talk about it, maybe I need to talk about her, maybe I need to talk about him. You know, I was as popular on the football team in high school as Ted Burton even though he *was* the star quarterback. All the girls had crushes on the team and they fed our huge egos. We loved it.

"Since Celeste was a cheerleader, why did it come as a surprise that she would fall for Burton? I knew how things went down, but I didn't want them to go that way with my sister for godsakes."

"I know…"

"I knew he was a player, and I'm not talking football here, but Celeste fell head over heels for him—nothing we said mattered. She was young and innocent until she met him. I should have put a stop to it, or at least tried to, but I was caught up in it like the rest of the team. Hell, it was the same story in every school—first loves, broken hearts. Guess that's what teenage years are about only my sister's story had a horrible ending. How I would love to go back and fix things."

"We can't, Michael. We can only wish something positive is learned and go on."

"I know. Sorry to start your day with this." She'd heard the story dozens of times over the years, but still listened patiently. Still remained supportive.

"No problem. You know the old saying, Sad start to day means happy ending at night."

"What?"

Rachel made a goofy face.

"You just made that up," he said as he started tickling her.

She squealed, begging him to stop.

"Okay, okay. We have a mess to clean up downstairs, don't we? Besides, I'm starved. What's the old saying about breakfast?"

"You're talking about that old Proverb: Full belly, glad heart."

"Right on, honey. You took the words right out of this hungry mouth."

Several weeks passed. Celeste, the mystery lady, didn't call the station again. No suicide reports came through the wire. Maybe the woman found peace.

Michael waited as Alex finished the news before turning back to his tribute honoring men and women serving in our military. It was a difficult show—hard on everyone. He had worked on it for over a month putting unbelievable stress on himself in the process. It was challenging to expose the horrors of war in front of parents who had lost children.

As Alex finished her update, Bob signaled to start. "Welcome back to our program honoring our country's military men and women. We appreciate your calls—"

Celeste's voice interrupted. "Michael, could you give me a

few minutes? You have a group of wonderful people with you tonight and I'm sure a lot of listeners are tuned in. I'd like to visit with them."

He flinched hoping it went unnoticed. He turned toward his guests. "Do you mind if I take this last call?" He waited for their nods before going on. "Of course I can give you time, Celeste. I haven't heard from you in awhile. How have you been?"

"Worried, Michael. The parents' stories touched my heart. I can relate to losing a child."

"You lost a child?"

"Yes."

"I'm sorry to hear that."

She was quiet for a moment. Then, "I'm here to share my worries."

"Please go on."

"Listening to these stories brought back many memories. My son's birth was difficult, but he was my miracle baby. Times were tough back then and I didn't have a family I could count on. I had to protect him—evil surrounded us. It was too strong and I ended up losing him."

"Just like some of the parents with us tonight who have lost their sons or daughters."

"That's right. The pain penetrates the soul."

"Of course."

"Michael, you're blessed to have three healthy, beautiful children."

Fear squeezed his heart. *How does she know I have three kids?*

One of the mothers interrupted. "Michael, may I say something to your caller?"

"Of course. Go ahead."

"My daughter died fighting for the freedom of our country. I'm sure I speak for everyone here in expressing sympathy for your loss."

Noticing Bob's signal to wrap, Michael thanked his guests and bid them goodnight.

"Celeste's voice floated through the studio. "Michael, I'm sorry for *your* family's loss."

The line went dead.

Michael kept his composure until his guests left the studio. Then he got up, throwing his earpiece on the desk. "She *has* been watching me. I never talk about my family on the air. We had dinner at Theo's last night. Was she there? Is she stalking us? What did she mean my family's loss?"

Bob made his way to Michael's desk. "Hold on, buddy, not so fast. You've jumped from a lonely woman who sounds a little mixed-up to a stalker."

"Hell, she said she was sorry for my family's loss. I think she means to hurt someone. It sounded like a threat."

Bob's face paled. His voice lowered as he put his hand on Michael's shoulder. "It's no secret in this town that your family lost a child." Bob saw the anguish in Michael's face as old memories surfaced.

Michael shook his head and sat down. His voice was slow and heavy with pain. "Yeah, right. My sister."

"We've been friends for a long time. You've covered your anguish through the years, but it's always there waiting to be exposed. As horrible as your loss, Mike, it made you a strong, compassionate man."

"Thanks, but dammit all to hell, she mentioned my children—she's getting too personal." He stood up, knocking his chair over, startling Bob. "Sorry, I didn't mean to go over the top."

"Man, why are you letting this caller get to you? It shocked me too when she mentioned your kids, but I think she relates to you like, you know, a kindred spirit. If you want to get the authorities involved, say the word and we'll do it. She's sending our ratings to the stars, but none of us want to jeopardize your family."

"I'm not sure what to do. If we get the police involved, she might panic and harm herself. At the same time, if we have her investigated, the media would have a field day with us. I can hear them—Michael Adams harassing one of his listeners, a sad, lonely woman, who lost her son in the war. Can you imagine what that would do to our ratings? She hasn't said anything menacing. No, I guess we have to give this more thought. The first thing we need to do is find out how she's getting air time."

"I agree. It's probably a glitch in our computers. Hell, one of the crew could be messing with us." Bob looked at Michael as a light bulb went off in his head. "Wait a minute, maybe this *is* internal—someone working behind the scenes to make fools of us—our competition. What do you think?"

"Anything is possible, but going along with your scenario for a moment, their plan backfired. Whoever is doing this hasn't hurt us."

Bob chuckled. "Yeah, you're right. The damn fools are helping us." His eyes widened, "Of course, the other alternative, our caller could be a raving, homicidal maniac."

"Could be," Mike said in a scary tone.

"Yeah, my imagination is working overtime. I'm sure she's just a lonely woman." Bob grinned. "No matter what—I'd love to meet her. You think she looks as good as she sounds?"

"Get your mind out of there."

"Oh, come on, buddy. Wouldn't you like to know where you could find a woman with a voice that seeps into your mind and soul?"

"I already have one. Let's call it a night and sleep on it."

Bob frowned. "Yeah, like we're going to get any sleep."

THREE

Michael rushed from work. He'd forgotten Rachel agreed to host one of the station's charity events at the country club. It would take twenty minutes to get there and make an appearance. He called—she was already at the club.

Rachel was special. He had known it the first time he saw her. It was love at first sight, if that's possible when you're five years old. He loved her in grade school, he loved her in high school when he tried to convince her to run away and get married, and by the time they got in college, his love was on the verge of hormonal lust. When she married him, it was the happiest day of his life.

Now, he not only thanked God every day for her, but he thanked God his family could live in small town USA away from big city crime. It was hard to realize that David, his youngest, was ten, going on twenty, Jennifer was twelve, the spitting image of Rachel at that age, and Christopher was approaching sixteen with a physique mimicking Michael's at that age. They were all involved in one thing or another and Rachel right along with them. He couldn't believe she had an open night for this event.

Pulling in front of the club, he maneuvered around the valet parking sign and tried to get close to his wife's car—impossible. He looked forward to spending time with Rachel and friends away from the station. He needed something other than the mysterious Celeste to think about, even though her voice had taken permanent residence in his head.

As soon as he stepped inside, he spotted Rachel in the center of the room laughing and talking to Rob Bennett. When Michael noticed Rob sliding his hand up and down Rachel's back, jealousy flared. He started walking toward her and saw relief on her face. She smiled and kissed him warmly before whispering "Thanks for rescuing me." She took his arm, moving him toward their friends.

He grabbed a drink off a tray as his son's assistant football coach grabbed him in a bear hug causing most of his drink to shower Tom's jacket.

"Sorry, man. I didn't mean to give you a bourbon bath."

"Better than any cologne I could put on." Tom grinned. "Hey, caught your show the other night—your ratings must be soaring."

"That's always a good thing."

"Come on, you know it's about that sweet sounding broad on your show."

Michael looked down. He didn't want to get into this. "I wouldn't call her a broad."

Rachel felt the tenseness and interrupted by putting her arm through Michael's. "Sorry to take him away, Tom, but we need to visit with the Mulligans."

Tom grabbed his arm again. "Hold on, you're not getting away that easy. We've all been speculating about that woman." He looked at Rachel.

"What's your take on her, Rach?"

"I feel sorry for her. She's obviously troubled and if talking with Michael can help, I'm glad."

Tom's wife walked up just then. "How can you *not* feel sorry for that woman? She lost a child in the damn war."

Kim chimed in, "Did she say her son died in the war?"

Michael spoke up. "I really don't know."

The group looked at each other not knowing what to say.

Rachel smiled. "I think she just needs someone to talk to." She looked toward the podium. "Oh, Michael, it's time for you to begin the auction."

Tom hit him on the back. "Better you than me, bud."

As Michael walked to the podium, some of his tension drifted away. *Maybe I am making too much of this. If the woman needs to talk, she's come to the right place. It's my job after all.*

Michael took the long way to work on Monday. He needed to concentrate on the upcoming broadcast regarding exploitation of children. When he got to the studio, Bob was pacing up and down waiting for him.

"Michael, I need to talk to you in the office."

After they were out of earshot, Bob said, "I guess I'm as paranoid as you, but listen to this. When I got in my office this morning, Alex was there rifling through papers on my desk."

Mike laughed. "It's your charm, Bob. Seriously, I wouldn't worry about her. You know as well as I do how ambitious she is. What would she have to gain by getting Celeste into our system? She's young and trying to climb that proverbial ladder of success. Maybe she wants a go at your job, or mine, who knows?"

"What did she expect to find on my desk?"

"No idea."

"Something else, Mike, she's always watching you. I think you need to be careful around her."

"What the hell are you talking about?"

"Talk around the water cooler—she's got a thing for you."

"Come on, man. Alex has asked me out to dinner a couple of times when we've worked late. That's it." He saw Bob's eyebrows arch. "Cut it out. Lots of guys around here would go for it, but I'm not one of them."

"Well, buddy, she *is* gorgeous. I'd like to see that mass of auburn hair spread out on a pillow next to mine. I'd like to feel its fire."

"Get real, man."

"I am. Wouldn't you like to look into those gold cat eyes? I'm serious—I'd like a piece of that."

"Okay, you've said enough. You're way too old for that gal."

"Well, I can dream, can't I? You, my friend, better watch your step."

"Warning noted. Now, can we get back to business? Is every-thing in place for our good doctor?"

"Yeah, and I hope your lady contacts you."

"Get off that, will you?" Michael glared at Bob. "I mean it—get off that 'your lady' business."

Alex slid from her chair like a man-eating tiger—her eyes never leaving her prey. She stood a short distance from Michael as he began his opening. She loved the way he picked up his intro so effortlessly, so professionally, so absolutely sexy. The corners of her lips turned upward as she fantasized that in a matter of minutes, he would look in her direction and gain impetus from seeing her. She wanted this man from the first time she saw him and she always got what she wanted.

Alex's bold gaze hit Michael in the gut. *Dear God, Bob was right. She wants me.* Michael covered his embarrassment by turn-ing toward the station manager as he ended his countdown. He was on.

"Ladies and gentlemen, welcome to a program dedicated to children and parents. We are fortunate to have knowledgeable guests with us tonight who will share their expertise in the con-stant fight against exploitation of children. Before we begin, I'd like to introduce Doctor Solomon Levy, a noted psychologist from UCLA, Harriet Abel and George Johns, AMC Organization, Ad-vocates for Missing Children, and James Hartford, an FBI agent.

"Let's begin with Mr. Hartford. Sir, would you describe a child abduction?"

"There are many ways to take a child. It's not necessarily like the old days where unsavory people haunted school grounds and parks looking for vulnerable children." He turned toward the other guests. "Don't misunderstand. These are still ripe places, but we can thank the internet for providing predators an easier connection."

"Thank you, Mr. Hartford." Michael turned toward Dr. Levy. "Doctor, I want to thank you and Miss Abel for your tireless work for exploited children."

Dr. Levy nodded at Miss Abel. "To know our work has helped even one child would be our greatest joy. Michael. Many children will bear the scars of their experiences for the rest of their lives. On the other hand, in time, countless children return to normal lives."

Dr. Levy looked at Hartford. "Sir, may I respond to your description of an abduction?"

"Of course."

"I'd like to add all parents *must* warn their children of strangers who lure their kids with pets or offering gifts such as ice cream, etc. Parents need to understand that once their children get involved with the dangerous characters we're discussing, their innocence could be destroyed forever."

All the guests shook their heads, commiserating with the doctor.

"Michael, Michael..."

The guests registered surprise.

"Welcome, Celeste." He turned to his guests to explain. "Celeste calls in frequently to join important discussions such as this."

Hartford smiled. "Michael, I imagine most of us have heard Celeste on your program."

"I appreciate your comment, Mr. Hartford. Now, Celeste, do you have a question?"

"Yes, but first, I'd like to express my gratitude to all your guests. I admire them for their dedication and willingness to help children. I would like to know what these particular organizations are doing to help the children they're discussing."

Michael nodded. "Miss Abel, Mr. Johns, would either, or both, of you like to take this question?"

Miss Abel spoke first. "The organization Mr. Johns and I represent, AMC, has volunteers from all over the world whose primary focus is to find lost children. We have done extensive research profiling abductors. Many are middle-aged white males with above average intelligence and usually have access to computers. The profiles show that child abductors come from all walks of life and can include all ages. We urge parents to exercise control over their children's internet activities."

Michael commented. "Folks, our guests need your help to continue their important work. Their contact numbers will be posted at the close of this program."

He turned to Mr. Johns. "Mr. Johns, would you like to add to this discussion?"

"I'd like to emphasize that child abductions produces many victims. It bears repeating that victims may be severely affected with unnecessary feelings of guilt and shame. We are here to remind them that they are the *victims.*

"Please keep in mind though that we are speaking in generalities—not specific cases."

Mr. Hartford, the FBI agent, cleared his throat. "The FBI's website on *Crimes Against Children* discusses abduction as well as exploitation of children in much more detail than I can do during this limited time. I encourage all listeners to check that site for more information."

Michael said, "My thanks to all our guests for their insights and now I invite our listeners to call in."

The first call came from a woman in Duluth. "I want to let your listeners know that a lot of kidnapped children are taken by family members. Mine was my uncle and I can tell you from experience that family ties confuse a child's mind."

"Thank you, caller. That took a lot of courage."

"Let's hear from Portland."

"I have been dealing with my daughter's horrible experience. I don't want to go into detail, but it's hell for the whole family. I'd like to thank everyone for their good work."

"Jersey, welcome."

"I'm a loyal listener, Michael. You've hit a raw nerve this time. I'm sitting here without my husband because he's in jail serving time for killing my son's abductor."

"I am so sorry—I don't know what to say."

"Atlanta."

"I'm exposed to this every day. I'm a counselor. I hear these sad stories—it sure plays with your head."

"Biloxi, you're on."

"This is for the lady in New Jersey. Your husband was a righteous man. Sometimes the Universe needs a little help getting rid of its garbage. Bless him."

"Now, let's hear from Los Angeles."

"Yeah, Jack here. Here's a shout out to the ladies in Jersey and Biloxi. What do you all think you are doing taking the law into your own hands? These people can be rehabilitated for godsakes. That's all I can say."

After taking a few more calls, Michael closed saying, "I wish we could go further with this important discussion, but our time is almost up. We will schedule a follow-up to this program. As I said before, a contact number for tonight's guests will be posted on EPOH's website."

Miss Abel motioned to Michael. "Before you close, I want to join Mr. Hartford in urging all your listeners to check the FBI's site, Crimes Against Children—I like to call them The Innocents."

Celeste broke in. "The Innocents—a perfect way to describe the children of the world."

Michael commented. "That's a good ending for this show, Celeste."

Michael closed the session repeating his promise to air a follow-up to this discussion in the near future.

As his guests were leaving, Michael stood, gathering his papers and heard, "Well done, Champion. Remember, 'Suffer the Little Children.'" He glanced around the studio. Apparently, no one else heard Celeste's whispered words, not even Bob.

FOUR

It took weeks and enough red tape to fill a silo for permission to broadcast from Follett Prison. Michael had wanted to interview Luke Claymore ever since he was convicted of multiple murders six months ago. His case captured the media's attention again after he attempted to get a book published with graphic descriptions of his horrific murders—blood money.

Michael and his crew were excited but anxious as they started the two-hour drive that would take them inside the maximum security prison. They eased tension by cracking jokes and talking about an upcoming marathon race. As their vans traveled the last five miles, they caught sight of the prison perched on a hill overlooking a vast amount of land—isolated from humanity, at least humanity outside its walls. Instead of a non-descript block of buildings surrounded by electric fencing, the place looked like a medieval fortress complete with openings at the top wide enough for rifles.

The van pulled up to the guard stand. Michael presented the necessary papers. The gates opened, allowing them to pass into Follett's alien world. The guard made it clear that all areas were restricted and they were not to venture beyond this section. They waited twenty minutes before a man appeared asking for Michael. He was told to come in by himself and speak with the warden. Then, he could inform his men of the required protocol.

After the crew was given the go-ahead, they loaded their recording equipment and made their way to the interview location.

As Michael passed through numerous checkpoints, he was overwhelmed by a sense of doom that permeated his steps. Movies portrayed isolation, despair, inevitable death or lifetimes of nothingness over and over in various films, but the portrayals didn't compare to the real thing.

The guard led Michael into a cold, gray, sterile room with nothing but a table and two chairs. It seemed like an eternity before Michael heard the clanging and shuffling of metal scraping the concrete floor. He looked up to see Luke Claymore, the convicted murderer.

The prisoner looked more like a college senior than a hardened criminal. Although his face brightened with a smile, it didn't hide the coldness that lay beneath—a coldness Michael wouldn't want to encounter outside these protected walls.

Luke told Michael up front he was excited to get his story out and wasted no time declaring pride in his murderous accomplishments—as proud as if he had won the Nobel Prize. Michael delved into his psyche and came up with the same egoism at every question. The man didn't regret killing, didn't proclaim his innocence, and didn't ask for sympathy. In his eyes, he was a big man, a man far above his fellow prisoners mentally and physically. In Michael's eyes, he was small, repulsive, a man damaged beyond belief.

After Luke's interview, Michael spoke with Warden Toby, as he preferred to be called. The warden described the inmates' days contrasting those in solitary confinement with those in general population. Toby said he would like to be quoted on air that there was no way a prisoner could escape this maximum security prison and none had tried during his twenty year tenure.

Michael left the prison yearning to breathe outside air. He couldn't wait to review the tapes and ready his script.

Michael and the crew were ready to air the prison segment by the following Monday.

Before the session ended, Bob advised Michael through his

earpiece that the call board was igniting like fireworks. He took a number of calls before…

"Michael, that was an interesting conversation you had with Luke. It's hard to believe he took four innocent lives and feels no remorse. It surprises me your listeners are mixed in their reactions."

Michael glanced at the control booth—Celeste was back.

"Welcome. What is it that surprises you?"

"It's hard to understand how some of your listeners continue to believe Luke can change and deserves another chance. What happened to the saying, 'an eye for an eye'? Don't you think Luke should die for his diabolical behavior instead of surviving in prison for the rest of his life? He didn't just kill four people, he destroyed the lives of their families and friends. Now, fear, sorrow, anger, and hate will walk with these people the rest of their lives."

"The death penalty is a controversial subject, Celeste. I understand what you're saying, but I think most of us want to find the good in everyone and give them a chance to make amends, a chance to change. I'm not sure I believe in 'an eye for an eye.'"

"Anyone who loses a loved one would disagree."

"Please, most people can't imagine something like that happening to someone they love."

"They *should*. Everyone *should*. You *should*."

His stomach dropped.

"*You* all need to try and feel the deep sadness that the victims' families undergo. Pull yourself into their skin and try to experience their sorrow, then you'll know monsters like Luke need to be punished in the harshest way possible."

"Celeste, I don't think we can play God and issue death sentences haphazardly. Some of us still respect the Ten Commandments."

"God! How dare you bring in God, His Laws. Didn't God give you free will? You are free to be good or evil."

"I am by no means a theologian."

"Michael, see what your listeners have to say."

"All right, callers. Any takers?"

It took a few minutes, then…

"Omaha. Get us started."

A man's gruff voice responded. "I was raised to believe in fire and brimstone and the idea never left me. Now I'm in my late years, so I pray the God of forgiveness is hanging around."

Michael chuckled. "That's the One I want looking after me too. Thanks for the call."

"Detroit, what do you think?"

"I may be the only one who believes this way, but I'm convinced there's a God of Fire and Brimstone. If I didn't—well, let's say I would have walked on the wild side and probably be dead by now dodging those fireballs."

"Different viewpoint, Detroit. Anyone agree? Kansas City, let's hear it."

"I'm glad I'm following that guy. I know what he means, man. I was raised on the streets and my old man, along with the nuns at school, kept pounding in my head that God was full of fire and brimstone. He always said if I didn't toe the mark, I'd find out how hot that fire felt."

"Albuquerque, go."

"God doesn't enjoy punishing us, Michael. We're just weak mortals after all. I think He'd much rather His creations repent of their wrongdoings and He could forgive them."

"Folks, I'll take one more call on this interesting topic."

"Reno, your opinion?"

"Why can't God be both? Just my view."

Bob encouraged him to stretch the time.

"Okay, the director gave me the go-ahead for more calls."

"Salem, you're on."

"Come on, Albuquerque. God doesn't enjoy punishing us. We punish ourselves. People analyze too much. If there is a God, I think He sits back and laughs at us for not taking charge of our own lives."

Celeste's voice chimed in. "Michael, don't forget you are free to punish evil and reward good. Can't you see that?"

"Celeste, don't get upset. I think we are going too far afield from the subject. Now—"

"I'm not finished, Michael." Her voice was edged with anger. "You have let the devil proliferate the world. If evil were taken out immediately, not given a chance to kill or harm again, my world would be so much better. You have the means to handle the evil, get rid of it, and you don't. You give in to evil, you give it chance after chance. How many innocents have died because a killer was given another opportunity? You have covered hatred, greed, and lust under the guise of certain sections of our society. Some of these people profit from urging citizens to love their brothers, forgive, and equal rights for all. Greed, dear friend."

Michael wanted to cut to commercial, but when he looked at Bob, he knew by the smile on his face and his hand tracing a circle, he should keep going.

"Again, I'm sorry you're upset, Celeste, and I apologize for bringing God into our discussion. May I say that God, the devil, and the death penalty are way too much controversy for me. The whole panel is flashing again—our listeners are anxious to get in a few words before we have to sign off. Let's take some more calls."

"Amanda from St. Louis. Welcome. What do you have to say about this?"

"I'm into forgiveness. I'm one of those people who believes everyone deserves a second chance. I want to add that I've listened to Celeste's comments before and she sounds like a woman of faith. I'm sure her faith will help her deal with her problems."

"Joe from Dallas, let's hear it."

"Way to go, Celeste. Damn good show, Michael."

"Time for one more caller, folks. Charlie, Pittsburgh."

"Love the show and love Celeste. I never thought too much about it before, but we do have free will and we're responsible for the laws. So, what do we do about all this?"

"Charlie, it would take greater minds than mine to answer you. In the meantime, we should all do our part, study the laws, join groups that are trying to correct this problem, get out and vote and put the right people on judicial benches. In other words, get active."

Celeste whispered. "Well said, Michael."

"Folks, it's time to say goodnight once again. Drive safely and stay well." Michael looked toward the control booth raising both thumbs in the air.

A few minutes later, Bob caught Michael at the elevator. "Great job, guy. I know you're worried about our lady, but she sure gets everyone's attention."

"I'm glad you said 'our lady' this time instead of 'my lady.' I'm still concerned about her, but damn, I have to admit she's good for the show."

Michael touched Bob's shoulder. "Wait a minute, are you sure you don't have something to do with this? It would be like you to pull this kind of stunt to get our ratings up."

"Get out of here! You know I don't pull stunts as far as the station goes and our ratings were good before she showed up."

"Sorry. You're right. Celeste has gotten into my head. She says things I'd like to but can't. All the time I was with that degenerate Luke I wanted him dead."

"Come on, Mike, you know it's the nature of the beast, every day we get immersed in sad, vile news. It hangs on like a coat of putrid slime. Bud, you're my hero, one of the strong ones, and you've always been able to hang that coat up at the end of the day."

"Thanks, but the older I get, the heavier that coat gets."

"Yeah, don't I know it."

Bob frantically waved papers in the air. "Mike, you need to return these calls."

"Who from?"

"One from Jim, your dad, the second from a cop, Mac something or other."

"Did he say what it was about?"

"No, said it was personal. Are you in some kind of trouble?"

Michael bit his bottom lip. "Well, last time I checked…"

"Okay, okay, just asking. Anyway, here's his number and he said call as soon as possible. Let me know if there's a problem."

Michael's stomach dropped. Had something happened to his mom? He rushed into the conference room, dialed the cop's number, and waited "Mac Hudson here."

"Officer, Michael Adams. What's happened?"

"Mr. Adams, I'm sorry if my call alarmed you. Have you spoken with your father?"

"Not yet. Your call scared the hell out of me. Why did you call my dad?"

"I'd rather not discuss it over the phone. I can tell you though it's about reopening your sister's case. I'd like to meet with you and your father. Why don't you call him and then call me back?"

"All right, Officer, I'll check with dad and get back to you."

In a matter of minutes, Michael returned Hudson's call.

"Okay, I spoke with my father and he said to listen to whatever you have to say."

"As I said, I want to discuss your sister's case."

"I know that much, but what do you want to discuss about Celeste?"

"I'd rather not do this over the phone."

Michael's heart tap danced again. "Officer, Detective…"

"Call me Mac."

"Okay, Mac it is. My sister disappeared a long time ago. I don't remember you as someone who worked on the case."

"That's because I didn't, but I'm interested in it now."

Michael took a deep breath. "Look, we've been disappointed time and time again—just talking about it tears me up."

"I'm aware of that, but wouldn't closure, any kind of closure, be worth it?"

"Are you saying you have new leads?"

"I'm not ready to say that yet. Are you and your father available in the morning around 9:30?"

"I'll call and check with him, but if so, we'd rather come

there. It'd be better to keep whatever this is between us for the time being."

"9:30 it is then—Jefferson Street Precinct. Do you know where we are?"

"I do and we'll see you then."

Michael spread his fingers apart, relieving the ache in his knuckles from gripping the phone. He replayed the officer's words in his head. *What could they have uncovered about Celeste after all this time?* He could hear the sadness in his dad's voice when he called. His parents still lived for the time his sister's disappearance would be solved or what they really prayed for—she would simply show up one day on their doorstep. He didn't like the prospect of them experiencing the agony all over again. They had such hopes for their daughter.

He turned as Bob came in the room.

"Buddy, all okay?"

"Yeah. The call was about my sister's case, but I'd rather you not say anything to anyone, and I mean *anyone,* about this. There's no need at this point for mother or Rachel to get upset over what will probably be nothing."

"Did they find her?" Bob hit his forehead. "Dummy. I'm sorry. I didn't mean to blurt that out."

"He didn't tell me anything. He just said he wanted to talk to me and my dad in person. So, we're going to the precinct tomorrow morning. Mum's the word, got it?"

"Of course, but what do you think they have?"

"Let's table it for now. It's late and I need to get out of here. I'll keep you posted."

Michael did what he could to convince his dad that Hudson's call was probably another lead that would go nowhere. He could hear the renewed sound of hope in his father's voice and he felt it too in the pit of his stomach, but he had to shield himself and his dad. If they had found Celeste, Hudson would have said so. He didn't see how she could be found after this length of time, but anything was possible. He steeled himself for the meeting with Hudson—he had to stay strong for his dad.

He gave Rachel a story about meeting a colleague and left for the precinct to meet with his father. His nerves were fried. *Maybe they had a lead on who... What am I thinking? We don't even know if something did happen to her. Maybe she just walked away from our family, or maybe she had a boyfriend no one knew about although I can't imagine that with the way our parents kept tabs on us.*

Michael and his dad arrived at the precinct at the same time. His father was fired up about the meeting, but Michael urged him to stay calm.

A young man's voice interrupted. "Sir, can I help you?"

Once Michael asked for Officer Hudson, mere minutes passed before they sat across from a guy that looked like he stepped out of GQ. It was hard to judge his age, he had a boyish face that looked like it never felt a razor's edge. After the usual amenities, Mac Hudson got right to it.

"Mr. Adams..."

"Make it Jim, please."

"Thanks. Jim, Michael, I want to inform you that I'm re-opening the Celeste Adams' case. I've been going over her disappearance and—"

Michael interrupted. "Forgive me, Officer, but why and who are you? If this is another trip down a dead end road, we'd rather not go there."

"Please hear me out. The *why* is—there are some things that have come to light recently that may have a connection to Celeste's case. The *who* is—I grew up here, but I have been living in New York for some time and transferred here a few months ago."

Michael couldn't hide his anxiety and he saw the same thing in his father's eyes.

"Listen, I can tell you're upset. I just want to let you know I'm working on this with Harry O'Donnell. Is this okay with you, Jim?"

"Yes, Mac. It makes me feel a helluva lot better if—"

"Maybe this isn't okay with me!" Michael interrupted.

"Easy, easy. How about something to drink and relaxing a little? Then, I'll put the reason I called both of you on the table."

"Sorry. Yeah, I'll have coffee, black. Dad, how about you?"

"Same here, thanks."

Mac walked around his desk. "Jim, the coffee is in the break room. If you don't mind waiting a few minutes, I'll take Michael down the hall and retrieve it." He tapped Michael on the shoulder. "Come on, walk with me."

Mac made small talk about Michael's work and, of course, brought up the mysterious caller everyone was talking about and how coincidental her name was Celeste.

"Hold on a minute. There's no coincidence going on here. She didn't act like she wanted to give her name. I'm the one who tagged her with that name."

"Was there a reason?"

Michael swelled with anger as he stopped in the hallway. "Is this why you wanted to see us—about the caller at the station? You think she's my sister?"

Mac didn't say a word—just pointed to the coffee machine. After filling three mugs, Mac steered Michael back down the hall and into his office. "Pal, you have to ease up and stop jumping to conclusions."

"Ease up? Hell, you ease up because I can't. You call us in here and now you're hinting that one of my show's callers could be my sister? No way in hell."

"Hey, I'm not hinting at anything."

Michael put his coffee on Mac's desk. "If this is why we're here, we're leaving."

Jim interrupted. "Son, settle down. Hear the man out."

Mac nodded. "Sit, please—this isn't about that. I understand you're upset, but if we're going to get anywhere, you have to let me have my say."

Michael slumped in his chair. "*You* have to understand that my whole family has agonized so many times about what could have happened to Celeste and about leads that go nowhere. It's been damn hard." He felt his dad's stern stare. "Okay, I'll keep quiet and listen."

"Deal. All right. I guess you've heard about the missing girl at Milford High."

Jim leaned across the desk. "Hell, yeah, I've been following that. She was a cheerleader like my girl."

Michael grabbed his dad's arm. "The girl made the news, but I missed the cheerleader part. Dad, you're on top of this, aren't you?"

"More than you know, son."

Mac listened to the two of them going back and forth. "Okay, folks, we're on it and there are a lot of similarities between this girl's disappearance and Celeste's. We're running a check on all the high schools in the area."

"Concord too?"

"Of course, and that brings us to Celeste."

"Mac, hold on a minute. My son goes to Concord and, believe me, I'm interested in everything that goes on there."

Mac nodded. "I know that, Michael. Now, what I tell you next must be kept confidential."

Mike and his dad exchanged looks.

Mac was silent a moment as tension intensified in the room. Then, he blurted out two words, "Ted Burton."

Jim Adams pounded his fist on Mac's desk. "What's that no good sonofabitch got to do with another missing girl?"

"Easy, dad, easy." Michael turned back to Mac.

"Connect the dots for us."

"I'm not saying Burton has something to do with the Milford girl, but he is a person of interest. That brings me to Celeste. I noticed in the file that they had some kind of relationship."

"Guess you could say they had a relationship. She thought she had something special going on with that guy, but I knew better. He was a womanizer even then. What's he up to now?"

"I can't go into specifics but…"

"The hell you can't. You called us in here to give information on this guy. Well, if we're going any further, we need information too. Looks to me like if you had anything on him at that time or now for that matter, he would have been arrested."

Mac laughed as he leaned back in his chair. "You're something else—guess you have a right to think that. As I said before, Burton is a person of interest."

Michael thumbed his fingers on Mac's desk.

"Michael. Let me get more than five words out at a time."

"Sorry."

"This is a probe investigation at this time and you know what they say, innocent until proven guilty. I can't tell you more than that, but Celeste's case could play here if things go down the way I think they will. This is why it's so important that you keep this to yourselves."

"Enough said. What can we tell you?"

"Jim, I need to know everything you or your son can remember about Ted and Celeste's relationship, dating, or whatever you want to call it."

Michael shifted in his chair. "It depends whose perspective you're coming from. If it's my sister's, she was in love with the guy—she wanted to marry him. From his perspective, he wanted to be with as many girls as he could, put as many notches in his belt as he could, and he damn sure didn't want to get married.

"Man, don't put us on that merry-go-round again. When we lost Celeste twenty-eight years ago, we went over all this with the cops. This is old news."

Mac met his gaze. "Yeah, but that was then and this is now. Was Celeste putting pressure on Burton to get married?"

"I don't know about that. She was a couple of years younger than him, but she would have left school in a heartbeat to be with him."

"I hate to ask, but did they have sex?"

Michael pressed his hands together, looking at his father. When he looked up, his color greyed. "Mac, if either of us had thought so at the time, we would have beaten him to a bloody pulp. Now, I'm not so sure. If I had to guess, I'd say yes."

"Any chance she could have been pregnant?"

Michael turned to his dad. "You don't have to hear this again."

"Yes, I do. I had to hear it then and I have to hear it now. If we can help in any way, we must."

Michael rubbed his dad's shoulder. "Right. Well, Mac, the other detectives asked us about that when she disappeared." He shook his head. "I can't say she wasn't pregnant. I *can* say she didn't look it. If my folks had thought that, Celeste would have caught hell. Dad?"

"You got that right."

Mac raised his eyebrows. "All the more reason for her to leave home, wouldn't you say?"

Michael leaned forward, "Maybe. What's happening with Ted these days?"

"Let's concentrate on your sister's relationship with Burton. Michael, tell me about your sister's comings and goings around the time she disappeared."

"Man, you don't ask easy questions. It's been twenty-eight years. It would be like me asking you what you did in 1982."

"Those numbers came out of you pretty easy."

"That date is branded in my brain. You think I had something to do with my sister's disappearance?"

"Hell, no, Michael. Sorry. I had to ask. I know it was a long time ago and not easy to think about, especially Ted with your sister, but I need you to try. Did you ever go on any dates with them?"

Michael chuckled in spite of the seriousness of their conversation. "Dates? You gotta be kidding. She was my kid sister and a double date with my sister was beneath me as a senior—know what I mean?" Seeing Mac nod, he went on. "I didn't like Ted dating her and I told him so. Of course, that didn't make any difference to him, or her for that matter. Ted was big man on campus, star football player, good looking, good dresser, and all that stuff. There weren't any girls at Concord who didn't want to date him.

Celeste was a cheerleader, you know, and that made her a prime target for our football jock."

"How often did Ted and Celeste go out?"

Michael leaned his head back and rolled it in a circle. "Let me see. Dad, correct me if I'm wrong, but when they first started going out, it was hot and heavy. Celeste tried for every night, but Mom put a quick stop to that. So, she went out with him on Friday nights and tried to sneak out on Saturday nights."

"This went on for how long?"

"I'd say about three months. After that, he started going with other girls and my sister found out."

"Did she confront him?"

"Of course, but he said she was too immature for him. Now that could have meant she didn't give him what he wanted—I don't know, but she came crying to me that her life was over, she'd never love again, and all the things young girls feel at that age. Hell, she was only fifteen." He stopped as memories coursed through his mind. "Mac, I have to tell you—even though I was a semi-big man on campus and didn't want to act like I cared about anything but football, it broke my heart to see my little sister go through this."

"Did you do anything about it?"

Michael took a deep breath and looked at his father. "Dad, you never knew about this but I did. I don't think it's relevant to what we're talking about though."

"It's all relevant. What did you do?"

"I beat the crap out of Ted, but he just laughed in my face and said I had a pitiful little trampy sister who didn't deserve him."

Jim smiled. "I did know about that. Your mom and I were more aware than you and your sister realized. Word gets around. I'll tell you this—if you hadn't done it, I would have. Come on, Mac, cut to the chase. We all thought that sonofabitch killed my daughter, but no one could prove it."

Michael looked surprised. "I had no idea you and mom felt like that."

"Well, son, you were in high school and we tried to protect you."

Mac nodded. "Ted Burton is a piece of work."

Michael gazed out the window. "You can say that again. Anyway, my sister was not trampy. She was an innocent young girl who fell head over heels in love with an upper-classman who was no-good. If she lost her virginity to that moron, I'm sorry about that, but what could I do? What could any of us do?"

Mac motioned toward their mugs. "More coffee?"

"No, full up." Michael crossed his legs. "After that, Celeste moped around the house. Dad, remember how you and mom had to threaten her within an inch of her life to even get her to go to school? She wouldn't eat, she wrote incessant notes she wouldn't let us see, and on and on. The only thing she wanted to do was go to cheerleading practice and chum around with one of her girl-friends. This lasted for about a month and then she was gone… just *gone*. No more notes, no more anything." Michael stared hard into Mac's eyes. "Okay, guess you can see I'm still bitter as hell. So, if I can help you nail Ted Burton, count me in."

Mac gave them a sympathetic smile. "Keep all this under your hats, but if you think of anything new on Burton, let me know." He slid his cards across the desk.

Cold sweat peppered Michael's forehead as he left the detective's office with his father. The thought of Ted Burton laying a hand on his sister made his skin crawl. He looked at his dad and knew what he was thinking. It would be horrible to live with the possibility your daughter could have been murdered all those years ago.

Michael maneuvered Jim to a nearby bench. He worried the strain might be too much for him. "Dad, relax. I'll be back in a second."

Michael went into the men's room and splashed cold water on his face, hoping to relieve nausea billowing in his stomach. As much as he hated Burton, his parents had to hate him more.

Jim Adams pushed himself up from the bench as soon as

Michael left the men's room. "Son, we need to talk."

"Yeah, we do. How about an early lunch someplace quiet?" Jim nodded.

"Follow me, dad."

Michael asked for a table toward the back of Vito's as his dad caught up on neighborhood news from his longtime friend, Sammy Vito.

"Son, I knew we would end up here."

"Your favorite place. Where else?"

"Yeah, good for this conversation if there has to be one. At least we're surrounded by old friends and happy memories."

"I can't believe you and mom suspected Burton of murdering Celeste."

"I'm sorry to say that's how we felt from the very beginning, but we couldn't prove it then and still can't unless Mac Hudson pulls a rabbit out of a hat. We didn't want to involve you any more than we had to. You were too young to bear the burden of this nightmare. I guess we should have talked about it before, but it was hard then and it still is."

"Damn, there's too much involved here. Think about it—Concord is where Chris goes to school and Burton's coaching the football team. Thank God, Becky goes to a private school." Michael noticed his dad's broad smile. "Wait a minute! You and mom made sure she went to St. Vincent's, didn't you? Dammit, you've been watching out for us. Where have I been? I feel like a fool."

"Mike, I'm your dad—it's my job to watch out for you and your family. You might not realize it, but good old Harry and I have kept an eye on Burton all these years."

"Harry O'Donnell? Harry, the cop Harry? Are you kidding? You and Harry—I can't believe it. Now I understand what Mac was talking about. Why didn't I know about this?"

"We had it covered. There was no need to worry you—you and Rachel were just starting out with your own lives. This was something I could take care of and needed to. Speaking of Harry,

I've been close to him and his family for many years. We can all thank God we've had Harry watching out for our safety and his brother, Father Andy, taking care of our spiritual side. What more could we want?"

"I want to get involved and I want you to start counting on me, too."

"Son, I've always counted on you—don't think I haven't, but you're right. It's time now for this old man to have some help."

"I don't know much about this Mac fellow, but there's something familiar about him. He said he used to live here. Did he look familiar to you?"

"Well, kind of. His name rang a bell too."

They finished their meal in silence each consumed with his own thoughts.

"I've got to get going, but if you hear anything, let me know, dad."

"Count on it."

Michael wanted to drive to Concord and look up that worthless piece of Burton shit, but if Mac Hudson was right about any of this, he had to act like he knew nothing. *That doesn't mean I can't quiz my son about how things are going with the football coach.* The only problem with that, he'd heard Chris say a million times that Burton could do no wrong. He understood where Chris was coming from. Hell, when he was on the team back in the day, he thought Coach Reardon hung the moon. Memories brought a smile to his face. That old man could work you until you thought you were taking your last breath and then work you some more. Too bad he wasn't still alive—he might shed some light on the slippery Ted.

When he pulled into the station's parking garage, he caught sight of Alex's backside as she went through the stairway/elevator entrance. He couldn't figure her out, but Bob was right—she was way too friendly around him. He made a mental note to set her up with one of his friends, maybe Tony.

He noticed Alex getting a cold drink in the lounge as he

passed. She looked up in time to see him. "Hey, Michael, you must have been right on my heels."

"Saw you going through the door."

"Why didn't you give me a yell? We could have shared an exciting elevator ride."

"Yeah, right."

"Anyway, I haven't seen much of you lately."

He responded with a sarcastic grin. "Just every day, Alex."

"I mean away from the news desk." She pulled a chair from one of the other tables. "If you have a few minutes, why don't you sit and we'll catch up?"

He shook his head. "Maybe next time."

"I don't bite, you know."

He turned toward her thinking this was as good a time as any to bring up a blind date with Tony. "On second thought, there *is* something I want to ask you."

Alex smiled broadly. "Ask me anything."

"I have this great buddy, Tony MacGuire, who I think you would hit it off with—"

"Stop right there. Are you trying to set me up?"

"I thought—"

"Well, you can stop thinking. I'm not interested."

"How do you know? You might be throwing away a great guy."

Alex covered his hand with hers. "Michael…"

He pulled away. "Now it's my turn to interrupt. Are you coming on to me?"

Her face reddened but cleared just as fast. "What if I am?"

"Don't go there. To tell the truth, Alex, even if I wasn't married, you're not my type."

Alex threw her hands in the air and pulled them back to lightly touch her chest. "How do you know until you try? You might enjoy yourself."

He stood pushing his chair aside. "Let's forget this conversation. We have to work together but that's all we will do together." He stopped at the door looking at her over his shoulder. "If you change your mind about meeting Tony, let me know."

"I won't, but if you change your mind about *me*, let *me* know."

As Michael rounded the corner headed to his office, he bumped into Bob and motioned him to follow.

"Well, partner, you were right about Alex."

"In what way?"

"She just made it clear she'd like to…"

"Say no more. I told you so. Did you set her straight?"

"Damn right. I offered to set her up with Tony MacGuire."

"You gotta be kidding. I bet she was mad as hell."

"Guess you could say that."

"Man, you've been out of circulation too long. Follow me here—she's hot to trot for you, she approaches you, you throw it back at her with an offer to date one of your friends."

"So?"

Bob shook his head. "Don't you know anything about women?"

"I think I do and probably more than you. What do you think of that?"

"Not much. How did you leave it with her?"

"I told her to let me know if she changed her mind about Tony."

"Is she going to act all bitchy?"

"If she does, who cares?"

FIVE

Mac Hudson's day started off like any other. He got to the station early, had coffee and doughnuts that would play hell with his weight, checked in with the upper echelon, and plunged into Burton's file again.

Mac thumbed through the material checking the yellow tags. Apparently, Burton graduated high school with a football scholarship to a nearby state university where he had a semi-successful career playing ball. When he came home, he applied for an assistant football coaching job at Concord. He was hired and has been there ever since—made full coach in '89. He had three marriages producing four children—one of whom lives with him and his current wife.

It looked like Burton had been involved in some questionable activities, but nothing stuck. He was the number one coach leading the number one football team in the district and that took care of everything.

Short hairs bristled on the back of Mac's neck. *Ted Burton, things are different now than they were back then. You might have been the golden boy of Concord High and I was just a geek, but this geek may fool you and everyone else.*

He looked through the glass surrounding his small cubicle at the hardworking cops who were his only family now. Mac leaned back in his chair. He tried not to dwell too much on the past, but his mother's words stayed with him. She hated cleaning other people's houses and always scrimping and saving to scrape enough money together just to put food on the table. She was a good woman and a good mother who never talked bad about his abusive father. He had no memory of his dad who abandoned him when he was a baby. He had to be a man like Ted Burton who didn't care for anyone but himself.

If it hadn't been for his mother's persistence that he get a good education, he would never have worked so hard to put himself through college, graduate in the top of his class, or go to law school. She dreamed he would become a successful attorney. She said so many times, "I don't want you to long for things you can't have, son. If you work hard and make something of yourself, you can have the world." He recalled the disappointment in her eyes when he left the prestigious law firm that hired him right after he passed the Bar and enrolled in the police academy. She couldn't understand why he wanted to get in the trenches and do his part to clean up the city.

He focused again on Burton's file. *Ted Burton, I need to put Celeste to rest so I can get a life. You're the reason she's gone. Damn you to hell.*

He thought Michael might recognize him, but why would he? During their Concord years, he was a horn-rimmed nerd who was always in Celeste's shadow, who tried to fight her battles around Concord, and look after her any way he could. After all these years his heart still ached for her. She was frozen in time and he was left with a timeless love. He threw his pencil across the room. He should have known she would never look twice at someone like him when she had a football star interested in her. *Why did she have to give her heart to Ted Burton—it should have belonged to me. Why couldn't she love me? If she had, she would still be here.*

How could her brother know, or Celeste either for that matter, that he sat in his home alone many nights and wished she would look at him like she did Burton? He laughed out loud. It's no wonder Michael didn't recognize him—that little scrawny kid had filled out to be a 6'4" man who pitched his glasses after laser surgery, drove a classic car and wore expensive suits. It took a few years after high school to come into his prime. After his picture appeared in the college paper, he was actually offered a few modeling jobs. They told him his square jaw, chiseled features, and athletic build made him a natural. He thought modeling was for sissies.

He thanked God he listened to his mother and devoted all his time and energy to his education. Sometimes he regretted not getting married, but now he didn't have much interest in it. One thing for sure, he was definitely tired of being the eligible guy everyone called when they needed an extra man to fill in. He could find his own woman if he was a mind to, but that would mean getting out of the precinct and putting himself on the scene, as his buddies called it. He had tried that a couple of months ago—went to what he thought would be a comfortable wine bar, but the crowd was too young. Even though he was only forty-three, this place made him feel like an old man.

Then, there was the time last week when one of the guys at the precinct set him up for a dinner date with a woman who had recently moved to the neighborhood. What a disaster. She was his age all right, but that was all they had in common. It turned out she didn't have much respect for law enforcement and that led to disagreements right away. The end of the date was a welcome relief.

Mac shook his head. The dating game wasn't what it was cracked up to be. How could it be when Celeste was his only love? What mattered now—he had to make sure Ted Burton got what he deserved.

He looked through Celeste Adams' file to check on the lead investigator at the time of her disappearance—Gil Hanson. Hanson was retired but still lived in the area. He dialed his number.

It didn't take long for him to answer. After Mac introduced himself and explained what he was digging into, Gil became defensive.

"Hey, back down. I'm not pointing fingers. This is a case I'm interested in, that's all, and between you and me, the young man who was a person of interest at that time appears to have been a busy boy in the years following the young woman's disappearance."

"In what way?"

Mac hesitated. Gil was old school—he needed a one-on-one with him to see where he was coming from. "Gil, if you're free for lunch, why don't we swap stories at Hilltop?"

"Tell you the truth, I don't get around too good—arthritis in the knees and hips, you know. You can come here if you like."

"Sorry to hear that. Hopping over fences and falling on concrete couldn't have helped."

"Got that right."

"Okay. Your address the same as in the file?"

"Yeah and bring a six-pack, why don't you?"

Gil wasn't much help. He looked at this case as a young girl who walked away from her family. Everyone involved agreed she was probably pregnant although the mother was adamant she wasn't. Gil confirmed the family's good standing in the community, and on and on. As far as Burton was concerned, Gil also confirmed he had a bad feeling about the young man at that time but nothing he could pin down. Burton appeared to be a healthy seventeen-year-old whose hormones were ricocheting all over the place. From reports of female students, Burton was the young man to be with. He could do no wrong in their eyes and the thought he could somehow be involved with Celeste Adams' disappearance was absurd. They weren't the only ones who thought so. No one at Concord High School, from the principal on down, was willing to believe he could be tied to the girl's disappearance.

Mac hated to see Gil's deterioration. The man had earned a number of commendations in his time. It was hard to see him so broken—the curse of police work? He didn't want to think so.

Mac shifted to an upright position. He had to focus on the present and take care of Celeste, even if it was 28 years later. He was glad Harry put the bug in his ear to pull Celeste Adams' material out of the inactive files.

Several days passed before Mac could join forces with John and Ed, two of the men working on the Adams' case. They transferred their frustrations to him.

"Hell, Mac, you know as well as we do that our hands get tied sometimes and this guy Burton skates every time. It's that old story about a good-looking man, and in Burton's case, a good-looking coach, with a bad boy image. Why the heck do women go for that kind of guy?"

Mac swung his legs up on his desk. "If only I had the answer to that one. Anyway, thanks for the input. Anything else on Burton?"

Ed replied. "He's one smug sonofabitch."

"I know that much. What else?"

"It's this way. If he was involved in Celeste Adams' disappearance, he had the balls to go on to college like nothing happened. There were no incidences reported during his college years that we know about. When he came back to Concord, well, you can trace his activities in the file."

"I talked to Gil Hanson the other day," Mac said.

"How is the old timer? Retired, right?

"Yeah, he's in bad physical shape now. To tell you the truth, I don't think he has much more to give up."

SIX

Michael took the station's last call of the evening. He looked up at the control room. "Over and out. I'm beat."

All he wanted to do was get out of there and go home. When he went into his office to collect a few things, he stopped short. Alex was sitting in his chair.

"Hey."

"Hey back, Alex. You need something?"

"You bet I do, but for now, I'll take you up on your offer for a date with your friend. He better be decent—or maybe not."

Michael swallowed hard. "Look, it's one thing to kid around about nothing in particular, but you don't kid well."

She moved closer. "Why, sir, I don't know what you mean."

"Cut the crap, Alex."

She flinched, stung by his words. "You don't have to be rude. I trust your friend has better manners."

Michael picked up his briefcase mumbling he'd let her know about Tony. He'd have to give this more thought. Maybe it wasn't a good idea to hook her up with a friend after all. He walked the stairs sure Alex wouldn't follow—she wasn't a stair type woman. When he got to the garage, there she was.

"You playing tag?"

"You *are* paranoid. You took the stairs, I took the elevator, and we arrived about the same time. So what?"

Perspiration slipped down Michael's forehead—a mixed blessing of stairs and anger. He stomped toward his car.

Alex followed close on his heels. "Hold on, let's get something straight. I like you, you know that, but you say I'm not your type. Okay, so be it." She extended her hand to shake. "Friends?"

He didn't want to touch her and didn't want to be friends, but what could it hurt? As soon as his hand was folded in hers, he didn't have to wonder what it would hurt. "Alex..."

She patted his hand before releasing it. "Relax. I don't mean anything—I'm just friendly. End of story."

Michael approached his car. "See you tomorrow."

She was by his side in no time. "Mike, you know you've never given me a ride in this classic? How about today? You know I'd look pretty good in this baby—the color will set off my hair and, after all, I'm as classy as it is."

"Leave it alone. I'm in a hurry."

As he watched her walk down the rows of parked vehicles, uneasiness spread through him. He didn't like where she was going with her provocative spikes. He admitted he was somewhat flattered when she first started. After all, a good-looking, savvy young woman interested in a man at least twenty years her senior. He was glad he had some appeal left for the younger generation, but he didn't want to play her game.

She's trying too hard. What is she up to? He'd have to keep an eye on Bob too since he made it clear he would jump in the playpen with Alex any time. As much as he thought of him, the man would be way out of his league with this hot number.

Bob caught up with Michael as he came through the station door the next day.

"Hey, man, did you hear the news?"

"What?"

"There's been a school shooting."

"Sweet Jesus, where?"

"This one's in our own back yard—some school in the burbs. Don't have all the facts."

Michael's phone interrupted.

Rachel's voice sounded tentative. "There's been a terrible shooting."

"Talk to me. Tell me it isn't Chris' school."

"It is. I'm on my way there now. Hurry, Mike."

He lowered the phone, his mind racing. What the hell was going on? It was far fetched, but could Burton have gotten wind that Celeste's case had been reopened? *It didn't make sense.*

He grabbed his keys and ran to his car. He scanned the radio trying to get news on the shooting. All he could see was his son in a pool of blood. He whispered aloud, "Dear God, get this out of my head. I lost my sister, don't let me lose my son."

As Michael pulled into Concord's parking area, he saw his station's van and numerous other news media. He dialed Rachel's cell. "Where are you, baby?"

She screamed into the phone. "Go to the cafeteria side of the school. I'll find you."

When Michael saw Rachel, he parked and ran to her as fast as he could. They held on to each other in desperation until she finally pulled back.

"Michael, you have to use your influence and get inside, even if it means wearing your reporter hat."

"How can I do that with my son in there?"

"You have to."

Michael told Rachel to stay put as he turned toward the news trucks.

"You gotta be kidding. No way I'm staying here—I'm going with you."

Michael saw Bob getting out of the station's van as the sickening whine of the ambulances sounded in the air.

"Mike, what the hell…"

"Bob, this is Chris' school."

Bob's face fell. "Damn, let's find out who's in charge here."

Michael looked around, panic filling his soul. Then he saw Harry O'Donnell standing close to where the ambulances were pulling up.

"Hold on, Bob, I see a cop friend. Come on, Rachel."

Harry saw Michael about the same time.

"Don't tell me they have you covering this story." He squeezed Rachel's hand. "I'm so sorry..." He stopped abruptly seeing the pain in Michael's face.

"Harry, you know we have a boy in there."

"I know—that's one reason I'm here."

Michael grabbed Harry shoulders. "I have to know—does this have anything to do with Burton?"

Harry glanced at Rachel. "Dear God, I hope not."

"Same here, but Burton is a loose cannon."

Rachel reacted. "What's this about Burton?"

Michael squeezed her arm. "Not now, Rachel. Harry, what do you have?"

"Not much at this point except casualties have been reported."

"Don't tell me that. My son and others I've known for years are... This can't be happening."

Harry's monitor beeped. "A call from inside, Michael. Hold on a minute." He turned for quiet. "Okay, hold on you two, they're bringing out the victims."

"Harry, what about the shooter?"

Harry looked at Michael and Rachel. "He's holed up in the cafeteria with some woman."

"Do you have a name?"

"No, everything's too crazy now. We're working on it."

"Harry, we need your help."

"I'll do what I can, but keep it to yourself..."

"You know I will, but I've got to know what's going on."

"Gotcha."

Michael silently thanked God for Harry. He had been a good friend to the family for as long as he could remember. Someone they could count on.

Michael's memories crashed as the police yelled orders over their loud speakers. "Everyone move back. Make room for the wounded."

The cop's voice continued on the loudspeaker, "Folks, this isn't easy for any of us, but the shooter is still at large in the cafeteria. The hostage group is trying to talk him out. It's imperative everyone stay back."

Michael watched as each child was brought to the waiting ambulances. He didn't recognize the first two, but the third sent a searing pain through his heart, Chris's best friend, Jon. Michael turned as he heard a woman screaming. Jon's mom looked at him with terrified eyes as she followed the stretcher with her son on it. He strained to see the others as they came out.

Then, there he was—the all too familiar blue striped shirt covered with blood, his face pale, no movement.

"My God, Rachel, there's Chris." She slumped in his arms as his own legs turned to rubber.

Harry grabbed both of them. "Hold on to me.

The news crew followed Michael suddenly realizing the lifeless young boy covered in blood was Michael Adams' son. One of the cameramen murmured a prayer.

As soon as they got to the ambulance, Harry moved Michael and Rachel back a few steps. He could tell Chris was gone. Michael didn't miss the looks exchanged between Harry and the medics. He looked at Rachel and the realization that their son was lifeless hit them at the same time. Rachel collapsed in his arms sobbing uncontrollably. He had to stay strong. It took all his strength to stay upright and he knew this was because of Harry's support.

Rachel pushed away and rushed toward the medic. "Do something for him. I can't lose my son."

Michael tried to move her back. "Baby, give them room."

"Don't leave us Chris. Someone, please help him. Look at all that blood—he's hurt, Michael. Chris is hurt. They need to help him."

"I know baby, I know." Michael tried to hold her in his arms, but she pushed away.

"Do something for godsakes. We can't lose our son." Rachel's words tore through his heart. The pain was unbearable. Michael prayed to God to take him instead.

The paramedics turned to Michael. "I'm sorry. We've lost him."

A medic working by the next stretcher turned and shouted. "Wait a minute, let me look at him."

Rachel grabbed his arm to steady herself. "Oh my God, Mike, that voice. What's going on? Why is she here?"

Michael scanned the crowd and saw Bob pushing his way toward them. Bob was breathless. "Michael, did you hear her? This is insane. Your son on a stretcher…and now, out of nowhere, that woman."

"Move aside, please. "Let me help with this child!" Everyone stared as the woman walked over to Chris and gently touched the shoulder of the attending paramedic. "It's okay, son, you did all you could. Let me help."

Michael wanted to scream—he wanted to tell everyone to keep that woman away from his boy, but he couldn't move, he couldn't speak. Time stopped. She leaned over Chris and lovingly touched his face before laying her hands on his chest. Everything moved in slow motion.

All eyes were riveted on Chris. The reporters from Michael's station sensed the tension and got as close as they could. Most of them recognized the woman's voice—no one could duplicate it.

Michael looked at the medic. A baseball cap shielded her face. He felt pressure on his shoulder from Bob's hand. Suddenly, they heard Chris take a deep breath, and then another before a pink blush flooded his cheeks.

Michael turned to Rachel but words froze in his throat.

"Michael, it's Celeste, the lady who's been calling your show." Michael struggled for air.

Rachel picked up Chris' hand and held it to her breast. Michael moved closer straining to see the woman's face. All he could see were her eyes. Eyes filled with gentle, calming love.

Michael gripped Rachel's arm tighter never taking his focus off the woman who just saved his son.

Celeste returned his look as well as Rachel's before saying, "There is no greater love than one who would give their life for their child."

They looked down at Chris in disbelief and then toward the woman, but she had disappeared, into the crowd.

Harry checked Chris's pulse. "It's weak but it's there." He looked at his friends, "I think we just witnessed a miracle."

Michael fell to his knees—it was more than his heart and body could handle.

When Michael opened his eyes, it took him a few minutes to realize he was in a hospital bed, an IV in his arm, and hooked up to a monitor. Then, in one horrible second he relived the shooting—the sadness, pain, confusion. He jerked his arm almost dislodging the IV.

"Rachel, where are you? Where's Chris?"

"I'm right here, honey. You have to calm down. Chris is recovering nicely. It's you we're worried about now."

"I'm fine, but I need to see Chris *now.*" He started to get up, but Bob managed to hold him down.

"You're not going anywhere, Mike. You need to get yourself healthy first."

Michael looked from Rachel to Bob. "What are you talking about and what are *you* doing here? Don't you have a station to run?"

"Rachel, take over. I don't think he knows what happened."

"What the hell is he talking about?" Michael barked.

"Honey, you have to take it easy. You suffered a heart attack at the school."

"No way. I'm a little weak, but come on, I'm too damn young to have a heart attack." As the words left his lips, his head spun. He closed his eyes before slipping into a deep sleep.

Michael saw Chris covered in blood. Someone shot him in

the heart. How could that happen? Why would someone want to shoot his son? He heard Rachel crying. I have to be strong... I have to protect my family.

"*I'm here for you, my friend.*"

Michael turned, "*That you Harry? What's going on? Come a little closer. Good Lord are those wings? I never noticed them before.*"

Harry laughed. "*Well, I usually keep them under my jacket, but hey, it's your dream so I'll let you see them. You know, everyone needs a guardian angel now and then. What can I do for you?*"

"*Chris needs my heart. Help me give it to him.*"

"*Are you sure you want to do that, Mike? It will be very painful and you can't live without your heart. Do you want to leave Rachel and the kids?*"

"*Rachel would get over losing me, but she would never get over losing her son. Please, Harry.*"

"*Okay, Mike, if you're sure.*"

Michael watched as Harry put his hands into his chest and pulled at his heart. Pain seared across his upper body. He screamed.

Michael awoke in a puddle of sweat with a nurse looking down at him.

"You're okay, Mr. Adams, just a bad dream."

He drifted off again.

When Rachel returned to Michael's room, she saw Bob dozing in the chair next to his bed. *Good ole Bob, he hasn't left Mike's side since this whole nightmare started.*

Bob shuffled. "Hey, Rachel. Our man is resting comfortably."

She motioned him to join her in the hall. "Bob, let's go down to the cafeteria for some coffee. Mike's dad is on his way to relieve us."

"How's Michael doing?"

"He had one hell of a nightmare a few minutes ago, but he's resting now. Coffee is a good idea. I need to stretch and we need to talk."

They added pie to the coffee and settled at a table next to a window. Bob tapped his fingers against the glass. "Rachel, my head is as foggy as the day. Look at the gray mist covering the top of that other hospital wing."

"Dismal, isn't it? I still can't believe any of this has happened. The day started out like any other, you know? Mike left for work and I took the kids to school. I planned do to a little shopping. When my cell phone rang, my world shattered. Nothing has been the same since."

"Jesus, Rachel, this is straight out of a Rod Serling episode, but we can thank God both your boys are out of the woods."

"Yes." Her voice trembled with emotion. "We have a lot to be thankful for."

"Listen, all hell is going to break loose tomorrow. The press is still at the school getting their pound of flesh on the shooter and his family, but tomorrow they'll be looking for new blood. Mike and Chris will be all over the news and that video of Chris with Celeste will be played over and over. I don't know what to make of the whole thing."

"Any news on the shooter's identity?"

Rachel looked up to see Harry coming their way.

She smiled, observing his kind face. Everything about the man was comforting—6'2", greying auburn hair, large brown eyes. Everyone kidded him he resembled a teddy bear. He didn't mind—a good look for a cop who worked with kids. He might be in his fifties, but he'd pass for much younger.

Bob pulled up a chair for him.

As soon as he got to the table, he gave Rachel a hug and shook Bob's hand. She felt a surge of relief hoping Harry could give them more news.

Bob got up and moved toward the door. "Sit, man, and talk to Rachel. I'll get more coffee."

Harry pulled his chair close to Rachel. "How are you holding up? I knew Mike was taken away in an ambulance, but I didn't know about his heart attack until a few minutes ago. God, what a day. How's he doing?"

"As well as can be expected. I don't think the enormity of the tragedy has hit him yet. He's pretty drugged up."

"That's not a bad thing."

Bob caught the end of the conversation. "What's not a bad thing?"

"That Mike's not totally aware of all the shit that came down today."

"Yeah, I wish this was a bad dream. So, Harry, give us the low-down."

"Apparently, the gunman was a jealous husband who thought his teacher wife was cheating on him. He held his wife hostage threatening to kill her. Eventually, a sharpshooter took him out. The bastard wanted to hurt his wife so he ended up shooting some of her students. Five kids wounded and two dead. Crazy world. The only good part of the day was that a friend, my friend, and his son lived.

"So, now it's your turn to fill me in on the mysterious woman."

Rachel stood. "While you bring Harry up-to-date on Celeste, I'm going to check on my men." She turned back to Harry. "Thanks for all your help today. Why don't you visit Mike when you finish your coffee?"

"Sure thing, honey. See you later."

They watched Rachel walk away, shoulders bent revealing the stress of the day.

Harry searched Bob's face. "Okay, man, what gives with this medic?"

"Guess you don't listen to Michael's show too often."

"Nope, workaholic."

"Well, this woman's called in for months. Somehow she cuts into the airwaves with that beautiful voice and gives her opinion on the subject of the day. We know she had a son who died, not sure how. She talks about how sad her world is and she cries out for help. The listeners love her. She generates a lot of sympathy. Our biggest concern has been that she might kill herself."

"What makes you think that?"

"She sounds so troubled. I don't know how to explain it, but when she calls, everything else fades away and we all hang on her every word. Hell, just like today, when we heard her voice, time stopped. Did you feel it, Harry?"

"Sure did—got my attention. It was kind of Sci-Fi like."

"Right, but this is the first time we've seen her, or sort of seen her. We don't know her actual name…"

"Then why are you calling her Celeste?"

"This probably sounds crazy, but she basically told Michael to call her anything he wanted. So, he tagged her Celeste. You know his sister's memory is always with him. Now, I don't know what to make of it. I actually thought Chris was dead."

"He *was* dead. Make no mistake about that. I've been around this kind of thing too long not to know."

"Sonofabitch, Harry. Why don't you scare the hell out of me? Are you telling me that this lady we call Celeste brought him back to life?"

"I told you at the scene. I think we witnessed a miracle."

"A miracle like in God…church?"

"That's right. God and miracles usually go hand in hand."

Bob put his head down on the table and moaned. "No one's going to believe this. God isn't very popular any more, know what I mean? What are we going to say to Mike? Can his heart handle this? Hell, for that matter, can mine?"

"Mike's a big boy. He'll handle it—after all, he has his son. That's all he will care about."

Bob turned his chair sideways. "You know, Harry, I'm not into this God stuff. I haven't been to church since I was a kid."

Harry stood pressing his fists on the table. He leaned down so he was eye to eye with Bob. "In my line of work, I'm very much into 'God stuff'. When people shoot at me, I hope God has my back. Come on, buddy, don't look so worried, miracles are good things. Let's go up, see Mike, and that kid of his." He slapped Bob on the back.

"Okay, but stop with this miracle stuff. It makes me nervous."

As they walked to the elevator, Bob rubbed his shoulder. "Damn, you're strong for an old guy."

Harry's baritone laugh filled the hallway.

Michael opened his eyes to see Harry coming through the door with Bob close on his heels. "Hey, man, get in here. You too, Bob. Rachel and dad are with Chris. There are some things I'd like to talk to you about while she's gone. I've been dozing and having the weirdest dreams. To tell the truth, I can't get a grasp on all that's happened. Maybe you two can fill in the blanks."

Harry pulled his chair close to Mike's bed and Bob slipped back into the easy chair.

"Mike, we're all exhausted. Tell you what, buddy. Get some shut-eye. I'll be here bright and early tomorrow and go over the whole damn day with you. I'll stop at the station before I come and get all the updates."

Bob brightened. He obviously wasn't looking forward to this discussion. "Sounds like a plan. I'm tired as hell too. What do you say, Mike?"

"Okay, okay. Maybe I won't be so groggy tomorrow. See you both in the morning."

"We'll stop by Chris' room and say goodnight to Rachel and your dad. Sleep well, my friend."

Michael tried to concentrate on the day, but his brain wouldn't cooperate. He fell asleep in seconds.

Rachel sent Mike's dad home with a warm hug. She couldn't have made it through this ordeal without Mike's parents—at least she knew their other kids were in good hands. She sat next to Chris' bed drinking in every aspect of his beautiful face. He still had that chubby cherub look. She remembered Mike's expression when Chris was born—he was so proud he had a son. It was special for him, but little did she know at the time how special a son would be to her. A terrible sadness washed over her when she thought again how close she came to losing both Chris and Mike.

Rachel took a deep breath, praying this could soon be put behind them. She wondered if anyone really knew what happened at Concord. Harry said it was a miracle. What memories that conjured up. In grade school at St. Vincent's, she read about miracles every day. She and her mother went to church each Sunday and Holy Day.

Her father had died young and her mother's freelance photography hadn't taken off yet. In the meantime, her mother worked part time for the church as a bookkeeper. Rachel loved spending time with the Sisters and helping them dust and wax the chapel—her favorite place. The aromas of lemon oil and soap still filled her nostrils. She would talk to the statues of the angels and saints and for the longest time she thought they talked back. She considered becoming a nun, but then other doors opened and she took a different path.

Rachel sighed. That was long ago and she lost interest in religion after her mom died. She looked for somebody to blame for her death and God took the rap. She was too young to know any better.

Today, when she looked at Chris covered in blood, thoughts of her mother filled her head. She needed her mom's arms around her, and her soft voice saying everything would be all right. Rachel recalled how much her mother had loved adventure and how they had traveled whenever they could—just the two of them with her mom's faithful companion, her camera, a gift from her husband. It made it special. She told Rachel when she looked through the lens it was like looking through her husband's eyes. He was there sharing all the incredible sights.

It only took a few years for people to realize her mother's talents. Margaret Benson worked magic with her camera. There was a time when you couldn't open a magazine without seeing one of her photographs—breathtaking views of faraway places or the face of a child that held the mysteries of the world.

All these years Rachel held back so many wonderful stories

she could have shared with her children, too painful. *What a fool I've been.*

Chris stirred, returning her to the present and allowing her to realize how tired she was. She closed her eyes whispering a prayer of thanks. Rachel knew she had a debt to pay, but for now, that secret would be tucked away in her heart. Sleep was welcome.

SEVEN

Harry tossed and turned all night. Images of the school children haunted him. All he could think about were the two families who would wake up in the morning faced with planning funerals. He closed his eyes seeing his mental scrapbook that overflowed with abused, battered, or dead children.

He pushed his head deeper into his pillow trying to think about something else. He could have had a family, but looking back he was glad he and Joan never married. They had thought about it, even got engaged for a few years. They both wanted kids, but decided it was hard enough protecting other people's. Marriage was tough, but two cops married? Damn near impossible. A good cop must stay focused—a family could be a distraction, at least for them.

He and Joan had stayed best friends, even had a romantic evening now and then, but always went home to their respective apartments where the horrors of their day stayed confined. Both were dedicated to their work and fit the old adage that 'someone had to do it.'

Harry had grown up in a close family. His dad was a fireman the whole neighborhood respected. He recalled how proud his parents were when his brother entered the seminary. He knew they were proud of him too, but they worried about him until the day they died. A cop and a priest, just what you would expect from a good Irish Catholic family. He stayed close to his brother, and they marveled from time to time at how their jobs intertwined.

Now, Andy would bury some of the kids he couldn't save, but they would be there together to comfort the families.

As children, Harry and his brother imitated knights in shining armor on huge white stallions. They would pretend they were on a quest to save the downtrodden and find the Holy Grail. For Harry, being a cop was as close as he could get to this. After all, he did carry a shiny badge and his car was white. Maybe his brother would find that Holy Grail someday.

Informing a parent that their child was harmed or dead was heart wrenching and with each instance a little piece of Harry's armor chipped off. When he saved a child, that old armor got a little of its sparkle back and made life worth living.

He rolled over and reached for his rosary on the nightstand— courage to face the day. He chuckled recalling what Bob said about "God stuff."

Damn, morning already—gray and cold. Once on his feet, he made a mental note to stop at the station for the latest updates on the shooting before heading to the hospital to report to Michael.

An hour later, Harry smelled snow in the air as he hurried across the parking lot and into the station. When he opened the door, the heavy scent of coffee rushed at him propelling him into the kitchen to get his first cup of adrenalin. Harry bumped into Mac in the hallway.

"Hold up. I know all about the shooting, Harry. I've got an appointment now, but if you need help, call me."

Harry was in the process of taking off his overcoat when Joan walked in. Even though he had his back turned, he knew it was her. He wanted to throw his arms around her but could only exchange a look they both understood. She squeezed his arm as she passed on her way to the chairs. She listened while the officers doled out an update on the wounded. He was relieved to hear the injured were out of the woods.

"Has anyone talked to the parents of the children who died?" he asked her.

"I did and your brother, Father Andrew, did too. He'll be

handling both funerals. The boys were best friends; their parents want joint services at St. Vincent's with Father Andy officiating."

Harry cracked his knuckles, looking out the window. "It will be damn hard on Andy to find the right words to piece together the shattered lives."

"I know it will, but we'll be there for support."

Sergeant O'Shea came through the door. "Listen, Harry, we've been swamped with calls on these kids. The media is hounding us for an update and the hospital is willing to give us a room for a news conference."

Harry moaned, "Okay, part of the job, isn't it?"

Harry looked at Joan. She had a smile on her face, but when their eyes locked, there was no hiding their shared pain. They were damn good actors—they had to be, but they could never fool each other. Joan often teased they were soul mates—he knew it when he first met her. They made a powerful team.

Joan looked at Harry. "Do you want me to go with you?"

"Not a bad idea. I could use some help handling the media and we haven't had a chance to talk about what happened yesterday. I'll fill you in on the ride to the hospital."

Harry gathered his papers and watched as Joan got her coat. He was relieved she'd be with him—she was good at managing tense situations. Her toughness surprised a lot of people. She was a beautiful, gentle woman, close to his age, but her long brown hair and big doe eyes fooled everyone. She was more than capable of swinging into action when needed.

Harry's eyes filled with admiration.

"Why are you looking at me like that?"

He walked to the door and shut it. "Because you're so damned good-looking and I don't tell you that enough. You are one tough cop even with that ponytail." He pulled the clip in her hair. "Of course, I prefer your hair down and…"

"Hold it right there, Mister."

When Harry stepped outside, a front was blowing through with nasty winds and cold rain. It took a few minutes before Joan made her way to his car. She wrapped her leather jacket close. He envied that jacket. As she got in, she flashed one of her beautiful smiles.

"Thanks for the heat. I think it's time to pull out the long johns."

"Too soon—just an early cold snap, but maybe it will be enough to keep the curious away from the hospital. We'll have our hands full dealing with the press. Are you up for it this morning? A beautiful woman can keep them civil, you know."

"You don't have to sweet-talk me, Harry. You're too close to this one. I'm ready.

Moments later, Harry pulled into the hospital parking lot and scanned the area. A flood of reporters camped out at the front door waiting for updates—he expected it. After all, school shootings made national news and this one was no exception. He drove around to the rear entrance—more reporters, but not as many.

"Joan, call the station and ask for more officers. The parents will need a protected entrance to come and go without being harassed. Even though these guys mean well, you know how it is."

"Done."

They made their way to the front door bracing for the onslaught of questions. It didn't take long. They were barely inside before arms shot in the air and voices raised.

"Officer O'Donnell, how about answering a few questions?"

Harry nodded. "If you will join me in Conference Room A, I will respond to as many questions as possible." Waiting for the press to settle down, he began. "I'd like to introduce Officer Joan Roberts who will be fielding most of your inquiries. Before we start, however, I'd like to make a statement. First, I ask your cooperation in respecting the privacy of the families. The latest update I have is the injured children are out of extensive care and all are expected to make full recoveries. As you know, we lost two wonderful young men from this community. Their families will let us know when and where their services will be held."

A reporter from one of the local newspapers raised his hand.

"What about Michael Adams and his son? We saw Mr. Adams collapse on the school grounds. What happened to him and what about his son?"

Harry squeezed Joan's shoulder signaling her to take the lead.

"Ladies and gentlemen, please have patience and I'll try to get to everyone."

Harry slipped out the door. He caught sight of Bob getting on the elevator and yelled at him to hold it. Harry gave him the once over.

"God, Bob, you look like hell."

"Yeah, right back at you. You don't look so good yourself."

Harry ran his hands through his hair. "I try."

"I should have shut my cell off and spent the night here. The press hounded me all night long."

"Sorry to hear that, but you shouldn't be surprised. After all, Mike is a celebrity in this town; everyone is interested in him and his family. His son getting shot is news enough, but shot at school, that's major. Face it. It goes along with your business."

Bob lowered his voice. "I know and it's a great news story, but it's different when a close friend is at the center of the crisis. I'm having trouble separating myself this time."

"You shouldn't have to. Let the station take care of this one without you. You need to be here for Michael and his family."

"Damn straight."

As the elevator stopped, Bob grabbed Harry's arm and pulled him to the side. "What the hell are we going to tell Michael?"

"The only thing we can—the truth as we know it."

Bob shrugged. "I'll let you handle that. Okay?"

"Sure, but back me up if I need it."

They hesitated at the open door to Michael's room. Rachel and Michael were watching the news.

"Hey, guys. Okay if we come in?"

Rachel stood, opening her arms for hugs. "You're just in time. This man of mine is driving me crazy. He thinks he's going home today. His dad's not here yet, so if you'll stay with him and keep him in bed, I'll go check on Chris."

She saw a look of concern on their faces. "No worries—Chris is doing great. As a matter of fact, I bet he thinks he's going home today too."

Laughter trailed her as she left the room.

Harry grinned as Michael tried to prop himself up in bed. "Having a little trouble there, my friend?"

"It's not funny. Man, I hate confinement. I need to help Rachel with Chris but looks like there's nothing I can do about it. Guys, pull some chairs closer to the bed. We need to talk."

All three sat in silence for a few minutes listening to a TV reporter talk about the shooting. Michael winced when his son's name was mentioned. Harry reached for the remote and turned it off.

"What the hell are you doing?"

"Enough of that for now. How are you feeling?"

"Wish I could say fine, but I can't. At least I'm not as groggy and doped up. They had me on some pretty strong stuff yesterday. I was so gone I dreamed you were an angel, Harry."

"No dream. I've been trying to tell you I'm a great guy for years."

"Yeah, yeah. Anyway, you had a great pair of wings. You know, being an angel and all...but what happened next really got to me."

"What was that?"

"Damned if I know why, but I asked you to help me give my heart to Chris."

"What the hell are you talking about?" Bob asked.

Michael looked at him. "I'm telling you that Harry started to pull my heart right out of my chest—the pain was excruciating." Michael's face paled as he leaned back on his pillow. "And you know what, guys? I meant it."

Bob leaned forward. "Meant what, Mike? You've lost me."

"I wanted Harry to give my heart to Chris."

Harry touched his shoulder. "Listen, pal, Bob's going to stay here with you. Get some rest and I'll be back before you know it. We'll talk more then."

Michael attempted a smile. "Sure, later."

As soon as Michael closed his eyes, Harry motioned Bob outside the room. "Let him sleep. I'd like to talk to Rachel about his condition. I don't think he's ready for all this yet. If you can stay with him now..."

"Take your time, Harry. I cleared my calendar—I'll be here until you get back."

"Hey, man, don't look so worried. While I'm gone, try to remember a prayer from your past." Harry poked Bob's chest. "I know there's one in there. Say it for Mike and the kids—it'll make you feel better."

Harry left Bob shaking his head. As he turned the corner, Rachel was getting off the elevator.

"Rach, how's Chris?"

"Fast asleep. The doctor assured me he's doing fine, considering."

"Let's go to the chapel and talk."

"I'd like that."

They opened the double wooden doors to warmth they both needed—candles burned on each side of the altar. The chapel was empty.

"Rachel, I'm glad we're alone and can talk above a whisper. Listen, I don't have to tell you that Michael wants to be brought up-to-date with all that's happened. Is it too soon to go there?"

Tears filled her eyes. "Thanks for being so considerate— you're a good friend. They aren't quite sure what happened to him yesterday. When they brought him in, the doctors thought he suffered a major heart attack, but after extensive testing, they couldn't find any damage to his heart. They have him under light sedation to keep a close watch on him for a day or two. Frankly, they're puzzled. Harry, God saved the two men in my life."

"I think so too. This is all good news. Mike's been under a lot of stress lately. Sometimes the body lets you know when it's had enough." Harry looked toward the altar. "I kind of like the idea of miracles…"

After a few silent minutes, Harry spoke. "Rach, okay if I talk to Mike when his head clears?"

"I'm counting on it. He should be feeling better later today."

"I'll walk back to the room with you."

"Sweet of you, but I'd like to sit here for a while." Rachel pulled a rosary from her pocket.

Harry started to get up when he noticed the beads. "Where did you get that?"

"I'm pretty sure your dad gave this to Michael years ago."

"Of course! I remember dad ordered rosaries from the Vatican when Andy was ordained. It seems a million years have passed since then. It's just like mine."

"I went home this morning to pack a few things for Michael and I found it in his briefcase. He always carries it with him when he travels—makes him feel safe. So, I thought I would bring it with me today. Holding it gives me peace. I hate to admit it, Harry, but it's been some time since I've prayed the rosary."

"You know, I was a little jealous that mom and dad put so much thought into those rosaries. Of course, how often do you have a son ordained? The type of bead was important—mom wanted green, a wee bit of Ireland, you know, and after some research, they settled on malachite. My mother discovered that in ancient folklore the stone was used to protect children from harm. The particular rosaries they chose were unusual because they were one-decade rosaries, a single bead for the "Our Father" and ten for the "Hail Mary's" instead of the usual five decades.

"Dad gave the rosaries to his friends like cigars he passed out when we were born." He smiled, a failed attempt at hiding his sadness. "Rachel, I miss my folks. If only…"

"Yes, Harry, if only."

He stood up slowly. "As much as I love talking to you, I've got to get back to work. You know I'm here for you and Michael. I'll check with you later."

Harry arrived at the coffee shop later than he wanted. He spotted Joan at one of the tables. He didn't miss the small wrinkle working its way across her forehead—a telltale sign she was worried. He held out his arms asking for a hug—to hell with policy.

"So, how did it go?"

"Same as always. Why do reporters always want to hear about blood and gore? If they had to deal with death every day like we do, they wouldn't be so eager to talk endlessly about it."

"Take it easy, Joan. It's the nature of the beast."

He saw her shudder. Death was too much a part of their lives. How many times she had told him death seemed to leak out of her pores and that the acid smell clung to her clothes. He knew she kept her shower area filled with sweet, fragrant potions that would wash away the stench.

Harry studied her face. "I tried to talk to Michael, but they're giving him sedatives to keep him quiet. Anyway, maybe we can talk by the afternoon. If you haven't eaten, let's grab a bite."

"Sounds good, I'm starving. You know how fending off reporters whets my appetite."

After Harry ordered soup and sandwiches, he waited for the waitress to leave before taking Joan's hand. "What say we save dessert for later?"

Joan smiled and touched his face. "You know, I haven't indulged in dessert for some time now. It would be a wonderful ending to this dismal day."

"Great, gives me something to look forward to."

After a hurried lunch, Harry went up to Michael's room sending Joan off to find the mysterious medic.

Harry came into Michael's room as Bob removed the lunch tray. Michael looked up with much clearer eyes than earlier. "Hey, my man, you missed some pretty good grub here. Want some?"

"No, I grabbed a bite with Joan. You look better, Mike. You too, Bob."

"Thanks. I'm on the mend. I think my head is finally on straight."

"Where's Rach?"

"She went home to get some rest. Dad is with Chris."

"Great, then we can talk." Harry moved a chair close to the bed. "I've got to get close and personal with you guys.

"Michael, how much do you remember about yesterday?"

"Every terrible moment leading up to my collapse. After that, everything's hazy."

"It's no wonder, buddy, you were in extreme pain when you went down. No one realized you were having a heart attack."

"Well, saying I had a heart attack is debatable. Apparently, they still don't know what happened to me."

"How about Chris? What have they told you about him?"

Michael took a deep breath. "That's an unbelievable story. When he arrived in the emergency room, the doctors thought he had been shot in the heart because of the hole in his chest and the large amount of blood he had lost." Michael's eyes teared. "Hold on a minute."

Harry gave him some water. "You don't have to go on. We can do this later."

"No, I want to talk about it now. Anyway, after the doctors opened Chris up, they could see the entry and exit wounds. By rights, the bullet should have gone straight through his heart. They told me they think it might have nicked a rib before it traveled through his body. So, that's what the doctors think—what do you guys make of it and was our lady really there?"

Bob responded. "She was there all right. Those of us standing close heard her voice—no mistaking it. I guess we sort of saw her, but couldn't see much of her face because of the baseball cap."

"Anyone talk to her?"

"No, she disappeared into the crowd. We were all too worried about you and Chris to follow her."

"Man, I panicked when I heard her and then saw her walking toward Chris. I tried screaming 'Stop her'...couldn't talk—I froze. I thought she might harm him, but it looks like she saved his life. I've watched the film over and over and still don't know what to make of it." He looked at Harry. "Why so quiet?"

"Just listening, I have a feeling the lady in question might remain a mystery."

"Why do you say that? Do you know something we don't?"

"No, just a hunch. So both of you know, Joan is looking for her as we speak. After Joan's investigation, we might have some answers on our mysterious medic.

"Mike, you said you watched the film. I haven't had a chance to see it yet. Tell me what you saw."

"If I tell you what happened, you'll think I'm crazy."

Bob responded. "No, he won't. This man already thinks a miracle saved Chris."

"You said that at the scene, didn't you, Harry?"

"I did and I meant it. Don't get upset, but when they brought Chris out of the school, I knew he was dead. I've seen this stuff too many times. I saw the medic do everything he could to bring him back."

"Rachel and I thought he was dead too." Michael's voice trembled. "You're absolutely right. Then, I saw the woman we call Celeste putting her hands on Chris and watched as life flowed into his lifeless body, back into our son." Michael covered his face with his hands. When he removed them, he had regained composure. "I'm telling you that anybody watching that tape will see it too. What the hell is going on? Am I losing my mind?"

"God, I hope not because if you are, we all are."

They heard a light knock before Father Andy came through the door.

Harry greeted him with a hug. "You remember Bob, don't you?"

"Of course."

Michael smiled warmly. "I've been thinking about you, Father. Maybe you can answer some questions for us. Pull up a chair."

"You look pretty good for a man who just suffered a heart attack, Mike. God must be in your corner."

Harry gave two thumbs up. "Andy, you're looking at another blessing. Michael's test showed no sign of a heart attack as they first thought."

"Wow, good news. Chris looked great too when I saw him this morning."

"Father, thanks for looking in on Chris. I don't know if you saw any of the news about what happened at the school."

"I didn't need to—I was there."

Harry looked surprised. "I didn't know you were there."

"Yes, one of my sad duties. I administered Last Rites to the boys that died at the scene."

Michael responded. "Did you see Chris?"

Andy stood putting his hands behind his back looking at the three men. "Yes, I witnessed the miracle."

No one said anything.

Bob stared at Michael and Harry in disbelief. "Come on, guys, this woman, this medic, no way did she bring Chris back to life. Don't look at me like that, Father Andy, I don't believe it. My question is, what are we going to tell everyone?"

Harry grinned at Bob. "Settle down, man, we don't owe anyone an explanation. Good God, why in hell are we worried about any of this? All that matters is that Michael and his son are living. Let anyone viewing the tape see and believe what they want."

"Right on, Harry. Who cares what they think?"

Michael glanced around the room. "I think we can all live with that."

Harry motioned toward the door. "I have to get back to police business. Good to see you looking better, Mike." He hugged Father Andy, "Talk to you later, little brother.

"Michael, I'll let you and Bob know if Joan finds out anything about your 'mystery medic'."

"Thanks, later."

Joan pulled up to the South Side Station confident she would either find the medic in question or at least the men could I.D. her. She didn't have much to go on except the woman had the body of a thirty year old, approximately 5'8", goldish hair—some said gold, some said brown—long enough to wear in a ponytail, had on an EMT uniform and a baseball cap. The media's tape clearly showed South Side's number on the ambulance. The camera couldn't focus on her face because of the cap.

As Joan opened South Side's door, the crew sat glued to the TV set where a reporter was going over and over the school shooting. One of the firemen interrupted, "How would you guys like to hear that voice from a woman leaning over you?"

"Cut it out, Tony. The kid was dying and all you can think about is that woman's voice."

"You've got me wrong, man. I'm just saying if you were injured and in the midst of all that chaos, wouldn't it be great to hear a voice like that?"

"*Sure* you were saying that."

After the news ended, it took a minute or two before anyone moved. That's when they saw Joan.

"Hello, I'm Officer Joan Roberts. I'm investigating the Concord shooting. Would you mind answering a few questions?"

The men pulled away leaving a nervous young man standing alone.

"Looks like I found my man."

He looked at her with a weary smile.

"Do you have time for a few questions?"

"If it won't take too long—I'm on my way home."

"I appreciate it. Look, I'll walk with you to your car and we'll talk on the way. I'm sorry, I don't know your name."

He grabbed his coat before going out the door. "I don't know where my manners are, Officer. I'm Jonathan Green."

"You did a wonderful job at the school."

"Well, I just did what I was taught. It's hard not to get caught up in the emotion, but guess you know about that being a cop and all."

Joan agreed. "It's never easy. Can you give me some information on the woman who helped you?"

He stopped walking and turned to her. "You're kidding. That's all we've been talking about—no one recognized her. She must have been from another area. My only suggestion would be to check with other stations that responded to the call. I'm sorry, but I'm bushed and need to get going."

"Thanks. Here's my card if you think of anything else. Go home now and get some rest."

As he headed for his car he turned, "Officer Roberts, please, if you find the lady, give me a call. I'd like to thank her."

"Will do."

EIGHT

Mac knew his reputation around the precinct—when he worked a new case, he was relentless. They were right. Celeste Adams had been a cold case far too long and he wanted to solve it more than any other he had ever worked. It was personal. Everything about Ted Burton shifted him into high gear, and if Burton had anything to do with Celeste's disappearance, Mac would find out.

Almost noon. He needed to grab a bite and get back to the station. He decided to take the long way around and visit his old neighborhood. *It's been a long time.* As he pulled in, that old feeling came back—same geek in a designer suit.

As he got out of the car, he scanned the parking lot—expensive cars had replaced the old jalopies. Mac wandered around the school grounds thinking of Celeste and happier times. Before long, he was at the football stadium. *It figures I would be drawn here.* He walked behind the bleachers recalling the area's reputation as a good place to make out. He wouldn't know since his high school days had been a big zero.

He passed the old refreshment booth and entered the stadium. He went up into the stands and sat. Mac looked at the field. He closed his eyes—he could smell the popcorn, hear the crowd. Concord had a damn good team during his high school days. Of course, the team was led by star quarterback Burton, who kept it No. 1. After Burton graduated, Concord went through a slump, only to become No. 1 again when Burton came back as head coach a few years later.

When Mac opened his eyes, he saw Celeste on the field looking beautiful in her cheerleading outfit, just as he remembered. He could swear they made eye contact and she smiled at him. He was filled with joy he hadn't felt in many years.

Then, joy was replaced by deep loneliness as her image faded.

It took a few moments before he could tear himself away. He started down the bleachers in a mindless fog.

He was startled by a whisper. "Mac...Mac...this way." A young woman was just disappearing among the trees some distance from the bleachers. He started to follow her. *"Mac..."*

He shouted, "What?" before running toward her. As he reached out, he came to an abrupt halt—face to face with a bulldozer.

Where the hell did she go? How did the dozer miss her?

The driver leaped down to make sure Mac was okay. When he asked about the girl, the guy looked at him like he was crazy.

Mac raised his hands in understanding and stepped back. It took a few minutes to compose himself. He surveyed the scene in front of him. The school's tennis courts were under demolition.

"Buddy, you okay? I gotta get back to work."

Michael's dazed eyes cleared. "Yeah, I'm fine, thanks." The driver turned to go. "Hold on a minute, what's going on here?"

"What the hell does it look like? I'm taking out the courts. Damn, they have to be over twenty years old."

Mac rubbed the back of his neck. "Right, that's what I thought." He started to walk away.

Then, it hit him—he could be looking at a crime scene. He needed to halt construction. The loud roar of the bulldozer pulled his attention back to the equipment. Landale Construction Company's number was on the side of one of the dozers. He dialed them asking for the manager in charge of the Concord project. A gruff voice rumbled through the line.

"Yeah, whatcha need?"

"Mac Hudson with the Police Department. Your name, sir?"

"Joe Robinson. Is there some kind of trouble?"

"I'm out at Concord High. It looks like your company is

tearing up the old cement tennis courts. I need you to put this job on hold."

"Don't know about that. You'd have to check with the school."

"We're investigating…"

"I don't know nothin' about any investigation."

"Mr. Robinson, check with your boss and see what can be done."

"Look, Mister Cop, I don't know what you're talking about and what's more, I don't give a damn. All I want to do is put the new courts in before snow flies."

"The area you're working—"

"I told you—my company doesn't want any part of what you're talking about. We have a contract—end of story."

Mac's temper flared. "Mr. Robinson, you don't have a choice here. You may be disturbing a crime scene. I can get a court order and we'll go from there if that's how you want to play it."

"Hold on. How long is your investigation going to take? I'm on a time schedule here, you know."

"I don't know how long it will take. You need to prepare for delays. Have your supervisor call me as soon as possible." Mac heard the phone slam. He couldn't blame the guy—time was money.

Mac's frustrations zoomed off the chart. He'd have to get a court order for Landale to cease and desist. It wouldn't be easy, but he had his ways. Then he'd have to cut through school administration red tape and that would be a nightmare. Time was a huge factor since Landale had already broken the surface.

A vibration in Mac's pocket signaled a call. *Damn, could it be the supervisor this quick?*

"Mac Hudson."

"Harry here, man. What are you up to?"

"I'm on Concord's grounds trying to get some information on the tennis court demolition."

"What the hell does that have to do with anything?"

A beep sounded in Mac's ear. "Another call coming in. I'll get back to you."

The supervisor's voice boomed over the phone—he wasn't happy. "Look, Officer...what is it? Hudson?"

"Correct."

"Well, what the hell is going on? I have a contract with Concord and I can't put it off."

"Your name, sir?"

"Lee Harris."

"It's this way, Mr. Harris. I understand your problem, but this is a police matter. I'd like your cooperation, but I don't need it to stop you."

Harris paused. "What's this about?"

"Sorry, confidential."

"Listen, Officer, my dad was a cop, so if you say it's important, I guess it's important. I'll help any way I can, but help us out here—time is money."

"I'll make it as easy as I can on you."

"I appreciate it. We put in the first courts twenty-eight years ago. New ones are long overdue."

"Thanks for your cooperation. I'll be in touch."

Harry answered Mac's call on the first ring.

Mac's excitement flowed through the line. "Sorry to put you off. I just talked to Landale's supervisor. He's agreed to cooperate with us."

"Hold on, Mac. What the hell's going on?"

"As I said, I talked to Landale's supervisor and he told me they put Concord's courts in twenty-eight years ago."

"Did you say twenty-eight?"

"Yeah. Harry, you thinking what I'm thinking?"

"Damn straight. You were in the right place at the right time. What the hell possessed you to go out to the school?"

"I went to lunch and on the way back to the station I decided to stop by my alma mater."

"What? You went to school there? News to me. By the way, how old are you?"

"Let me make this easy for you, Harry. I went to school with Celeste. I thought you knew that."

"Well, I am a detective—guess I should have. How well did you know her?"

Silence.

"Mac, did you hear me?"

"Umm, not as well as I wanted to."

"What the hell does that mean?"

Mac exploded. "That means it's not any of your damn business."

"Whoa, man. Simmer down. Should you be working this case?"

"Harry, give me some credit. Stay with me on this."

"Try and get rid of me."

Mac threw papers in his briefcase and made his way to the hospital to check on Michael and his family. He understood Michael not wanting to involve Rachel in reopening Celeste's case until they had more information, but he had to talk to him about this new development.

The hospital's elevator door opened on the fifth floor to sterility Mac hated and respected at the same time. His mother had been a patient here before she passed away, and while the staff had been kind and professional, the all too familiar odors drifting in the air were sad reminders. Even though several years had passed, it wasn't near long enough to fade the memories of her last days. As he stepped out of the elevator admonishing himself for his weakness, he saw Harry coming around the corner.

"Glad you're still here, Harry."

"How's it going, Mac?"

"Well, it's going—about all I can say. Is there some place we can have some privacy?"

"Let's go to the chapel. If someone is there, we can go outside to the garden area."

The men were silent as they descended to the second floor.

When they opened the chapel doors to empty pews, they smiled. Mac swiped at Harry's arm.

"Man, we're living right. Listen, before we get into anything, tell me how Michael and his family are doing."

"As well as can be expected."

"When I first heard about the shooting, I thought Burton might be involved. Don't ask why, no good reason. I was relieved he wasn't. Maybe I want to save him to pay for Mike's sister. Hell, I don't know."

"Same here."

Mac paced in front of the altar. "I don't mind telling you that all this is blowing my mind. I need your input."

"Talk to me."

Mac stared hard at Harry before turning toward the altar and gripping the railing. When he spoke, his voice wavered. "This whole situation about Celeste is so close to home. You know what the twenty-eight years could mean, don't you?"

"I know, but we're jumping the gun here. Our suspicions are just that—suspicions, but if they pan out, it could be closure for the family."

"The reason I came to the hospital this afternoon was to talk to Michael and Rachel about Celeste. I need you to tell me if they can handle it."

"Hell, yeah. They're strong."

"Bring me up-to-date on the shooting. I've heard rumors about some kind of miracle by one of the ambulance people. What's that about?"

Harry looked into Mac's eyes without saying anything for a few minutes. "I'm a deeply religious man…"

"I know you are and I'm sorry to say I'm less of one."

"Well, even so, if I hadn't been there to witness what happened, it would be hard for me to accept. But, man, I tell you, it *was* a miracle—that I'm sure of."

"So, what happened?"

"Michael's son stopped breathing. The medics said they had

done everything they could for him and it was over. Then, another medic stepped in and asked to take a look at him."

"And?"

"And she examined him and he started breathing."

"Come on, Harry, with all the new medical devices they have now..."

"Well, the only device she used was her hands."

"Who is this woman? I'd like to talk to her."

"So would I and a hundred reporters. She simply wasn't there when we recovered from the shock. So far we haven't been able to find her."

Mac rolled his eyes. "That's quite a story. How about Michael? I heard he had a heart attack."

"The jury's still out on that one. We should know something today."

"Here's the thing, Harry. I need to talk to Michael about his sister's case."

"Not a good idea today. There's something you should know. Mike discussed your reopening Celeste's case with me and he's determined that you call it off."

Mac frowned at the stumbling block. "Without even asking why, you know I can't do that. Doesn't he realize there's more than his sister involved here?"

"All I know at this point is that he can't think about anything but his son."

"I understand, but you know better than anyone else, this is an official investigation. His sister's case was never closed and now we have the Milford High case that looks like it might dovetail with Celeste's."

"I know that, Mac. Anyway, message delivered."

"When do you think I can talk to Mike and Rachel?"

"Let's see what the doc says."

"Okay. How about you and I sitting down over some coffee and going over a few things?"

"You got it. Do you want to poke your head into Michael's room?"

"Yeah, but is Rachel there?"

"When I left a few minutes ago, she wasn't. Is Rachel a problem?" Harry asked.

"The thing is, Michael didn't want her to know we've reopened his sister's case. This is one of the things I need to talk to him about. Everything is kicking into high gear and she needs to know."

Harry's concern creased his forehead. "Gotcha. Here's what you do. Stick your head into the room, pass on encouraging words, and tell Michael you'll see him in the next day or two. How's that?"

"Will do. Do you want to meet me somewhere around here or back at the precinct? You know we'd have a better chance of getting a good cup of coffee around here."

"You got that right. Listen, there's a little café, I think it's called Indigo's, about two blocks down. If you get there before me, grab a table at the back where it's quiet."

NINE

Alex watched Mac close the door to Michael's hospital room. *Who the hell is that good-looking Adonis? I'll have to check him out.* She had to see Michael and she had to see him alone. Rachel seldom left Michael's side and when she did, someone else went in. She turned toward the reflective elevator doors. She looked good in her clinging green sweater and short mini skirt. She wanted Michael to think so too.

Ten minutes passed before Mac came out. She scanned the hallway. Seeing no one, Alex ran into the room.

"Good morning, Michael."

Alex watched Michael turn her direction with a direct probing stare.

"Good morning to you, Alex."

"How about a happy look. You could pretend you're pleased to see me."

"I'm just surprised. What brings you here?"

She smiled. "You can't frighten me away with that stern look, love. What I'm doing here is seeing you." She took his hand and placed it next to her heart. "I care about you, Michael, and I've been sick with worry."

He pulled his hand away as Rachel walked in.

Alex quickly compared this so-called perfect wife to herself. She didn't know how Michael could be interested in such a plain woman. She remembered hearing that Rachel was a classic beauty. Some people might think so, but she didn't look too exciting to her. She didn't miss Rachel giving her the once-over.

Obviously, the woman had heard rumors. It didn't matter, but what did matter was the expression in Michael's eyes. Apparently, his wife looked good to him.

Rachel broke the silence. "Hello. It's Alex, isn't it?"

"That's what they call me every night on EPOH."

Alex smiled inwardly as she watched Rachel bristle and show a small moment of doubt in her eyes.

"Actually, I came by to see how our boy is doing. You don't mind, do you?"

"Of course not, Alex. As you can see, our boy looks pretty good, everything considered."

Michael shifted in the bed tugging at the pillows that had dropped down too low. Alex reached to help as Rachel came up on the other side and raised the pillows with a small fluff.

"Look, ladies, you're talking like I can't hear you." He reached for Rachel's hand. "As you can see, Alex, I have all I need right here."

"I'm sure."

"Is there something specifically you dropped by for?"

Alex dropped her eyes to hide their smoldering. "No, nothing except to see how you're doing. We work together every day, or have you forgotten? I've been concerned and wanted to see with my own eyes that you're okay."

"I appreciate it, but..."

"On second thought, there is something I've been tossing around. I was thinking..."

"Dangerous, Alex."

"Very funny. Anyway, what about taping a segment from your room? I'm sure Bob could arrange it."

Michael cringed. "I don't know. Broadcast from the hospital?"

"It's been done before. Your adoring public misses you. You know they want to hear for themselves that you're okay."

He turned toward Rachel. "What do you think, sweetie?"

Alex interrupted. "I'm sure your wife wouldn't want to interfere with station business."

Rachel smiled. Alex's infatuation with Michael wasn't subtle.

"Of course I wouldn't want to interfere, but guess you don't understand that Michael *likes* my input." Rachel took Michael's hand. "Maybe we need to talk about it, my dear."

"'My dear?'" Alex shuddered visibly. "You two sound like some old married couple. Where's the sparkle?"

"The sparkle?" Michael smiled broadly. "Believe me, the sparkle is brighter than ever. Now, let's talk a little more about your idea. Have you run it by Bob?"

"No, I wanted to talk to you first. Here's how I see it. Once things calm down a bit after the shooting and your collapse..."

"My collapse? Come on. You're saying you want to broadcast from here to boost ratings?"

Alex backed away from the bed with her hands raised. "Hold on. It's just an idea, but I guess you're right. I would do almost anything to boost ratings."

Rachel couldn't resist, "Anything?"

Alex didn't mind sparring. "I said *almost* anything. By the way, was that your mystery lady at the shooting?"

"You tell me, Alex. What do you think?"

"Had to be—there's only one voice like that."

Alex moved close to Michael, extending her hand to Rachel. She thought she had seen doubt in Rachel's eyes earlier, but now she only saw a confident woman supported by a loving husband. She realized she would have to scrap any plans she might have for Michael Adams.

She put on a gracious face, suddenly embarrassed by her tight sweater and skirt. "Mrs. Adams, it was good to see you, even under these circumstances." She glanced at Michael. "He talks about you all the time. Guess it's time for me to go."

"Good to see you too, Alex."

"Think about my proposal and if you give the go-ahead, we'll set it up."

Alex moved quickly down the hall toward the elevator. Anger bubbled in her like boiling water. *The nerve of that woman. In fact, the nerve of Michael too. I go there in good faith trying to see a friend.* She turned the knob on the water fountain hoping to swallow her anger when the elevator opened and Bob stepped out.

His face lit up. "Why, hello darlin'."

"Darlin? Have you been drinking?"

"Sorry, guess I lost my head."

"You got that right. Bob, if you have a minute, why don't we grab a cup of coffee in the cafeteria?"

"We can go some place better if you want."

Alex patted his arm. "The cafeteria is fine."

After she put her idea on the table, Bob couldn't hide his excitement. "Great concept. When I see Michael I'll go over some things with him and if he wants to do it, we can decide on a date."

"Fine, but the sooner the better." Alex paused. "Bob, don't let Rachel run interference here."

"Interference?"

"Yes. When I presented my idea to Michael a few minutes ago, he seemed determined to get her opinion."

"Nothing unusual about that."

"Well, it is to me. This is station business not husband and wife business." She hesitated. "Oh, never mind. Guess I don't like outsiders interfering, although she might go for the idea."

Bob leaned back in his chair staring intently at Alex. "Look, first of all, Rachel is not an outsider. It would be a lot easier on you if you would accept that Michael and Rachel are tight and always will be. They have the kind of marriage I would give my eyeteeth for—they're best friends, lovers, and value each other above everything else."

Alex's face reddened. "You sound like an ad to promote Michael and Rachel's perfect marriage. By the way, what do you mean by easier on me?"

"It's no secret you'd like to get in Michael's...forget it, not important."

"What's it to you anyway?"

"I think you'd like to have an affair with my man. Do you deny it?"

"No, as a matter of fact, I don't. I know you're friends with both of them, but honestly, I don't see what he sees in her."

"He sees plenty and you'll never change that."

"Don't be so sure, but I have to admit she put up a roadblock today."

"Alex, watch your step. Let's table this discussion for now. Why don't you come in a little early tomorrow and we'll put together a plan for the hospital broadcast."

"You got a date."

"Speaking of dates…"

Alex stood, pulling down her mini-skirt that looked like it had no place to go but up.

"Don't go there, Bob."

Bob was annoyed with Alex. If she'd accept how solid Michael and Rachel were, maybe she'd start seeing him. So he didn't have thick black hair like Michael, but his steel grey hair, even though it had thinned a bit, gave him a distinguished look. He didn't have Michael's dreamy eyes, but he did have hazel eyes that changed color to match his shirt. He was a little heftier around the middle than Michael, but after all, he was somewhat older. At this stage in his life, he'd know how to treat a woman like Alex. He decided to work harder at getting her to notice him.

When his wife passed away, he had been devastated. Loneliness still closed in at times and he didn't know what to do about it. This was one of those times.

He opened Michael's door slowly, hesitant to interfere with Rachel's visit. She spread herself so thin between son and husband, but her face showed pleasure. "Bob, come in, friend."

"Am I interrupting?"

Michael grinned boyishly. "Of course, but come in anyway."

After the usual how are you feeling and what's the latest from the doc, Bob went over his conversation with Alex. "Did she tell you her idea?"

"Sure did. What do you think about it?"

"I'm torn. We're talking life and death situations here. We have the families of two dead boys to consider. We don't want to appear ghoulish."

"I understand that and I agree. Let's think about doing a short broadcast to honor the victims."

"We'll work on it."

Bob moved toward the door.

"What's your rush, man? I want to talk to you about Alex."

"What about her?" Bob asked. "She's not usually your favorite subject."

"She's pushing again and I don't like it."

Rachel patted his shoulder. "Come on, let her be."

"Let her be? Hell, I've tried that, I've tried telling her to back off. I've tried setting her up with a buddy. I've tried everything and I'm through with all that crap."

Bob shuffled around the other side of the bed. "I'd like to have her interested in me, know what I mean?"

"Buddy, there's someone out there for you and she's not it."

"Maybe, but you can't blame a fellow for wishing. Anyway, enough. Let me know what the doc says. I'm out of here."

TEN

Harry waited for Mac at Indigo's. The place was almost empty, and it would be a while before the lunch crowd poured in.

Mac rushed in with apologies for his lateness. "Harry, I'm glad we can talk away from the precinct."

"Same here." He scrutinized Mac's face—dark circles under his eyes and the look of dread in them. *This boy is too close to this case. I should have realized it before—maybe I'm too close as well.* "This is getting to you, isn't it?"

Mac looked down while shaking his head. "I'm starting to think it's a mistake to dig up the past."

"Working with cold cases is your job."

"I know, I know, but Michael's sister was just fifteen for godsakes. She had her whole life ahead of her. She should be married now and have kids of her own making some lucky man very happy."

Harry nodded at the waitress as she set coffee on the table.

"Mac, I know that tearing this deep wound open after all these years is going to hurt a lot of people like hell. Think about it. I hate to keep repeating myself, but I will—it's been twenty-eight years since Celeste disappeared."

Harry sipped his coffee not taking his eyes off of Mac as he talked. *Damn, this man was in love with Celeste. How did old Gil miss this kid during the first investigation?*

"Mac, are you listening?"

"Yeah, sure."

"I'm sorry you're involved in this case. I didn't realize you knew Celeste so well."

Mac didn't hide his agitation as he met Harry's probing eyes.

"Harry, what the hell does it matter how well I knew her? I can handle it. I just want to give her some peace."

"You mean give her family some peace?"

"Yeah, dammit, put it to rest."

"Cool down, man, this is no way to show me you can handle it."

"Okay, I'm fine. Can I get on with this?" Mac asked sharply.

"Go on—I'm all ears."

"You know what we talked about on the phone the other day?"

"You bet I do—twenty-eight years. I can't get it out of my head. Like I said, you were at the right place at the right time."

"This might be the missing piece, Harry."

"You know we have to inform Michael's family about this and that brings us back to opening an old wound. Rachel needs to know about it too although she is fairly insulated right now. She's staying at the hospital around the clock and her world consists of Michael's room, her son's room, the chapel, and the cafeteria."

"What are you saying?"

"I'm saying, I know you're tired hearing it, wait a few more days before talking to Michael. He's fighting for a quick recovery; he doesn't need anything else to worry about."

"All right. I'll hold off a few more days, but we need his input." Mac pushed his coffee cup aside. "Have time for a bite?"

"I don't—wish I did. Anything else?"

"Even though I got the construction company to stop, I still need to fill out papers to get H&H on the job."

"Yeah. I haven't dealt with them in a while. Let me know when they're on board."

As Harry drove away from the restaurant, Mac's face played in his head. *I should have connected him with Celeste, but why in hell didn't he tell me up front he knew her?* He gave Mike's dad a quick call.

"Jim, Harry here, where are you?"

"Something happen?"

"No, sorry if I alarmed you. Are you at the hospital?"

"Just getting ready to leave. What's on your mind?"

"Can you meet me at Joe's Tavern around one tomorrow? You know where it is—over on Wellington Avenue?"

Harry knew Jim would worry about their meeting. Even though he didn't say anything was wrong, maybe he should have told him the meeting was about Mac. If he had, Jim wouldn't think there was another blip on the family screen. After all, Jim's family had all been through hell stressing over Michael and Chris and the other kids caught in the shooting. He had tried to assure him yesterday nothing was wrong, but he felt certain the family patriarch still worried through the night.

As he pulled into the tavern's parking area, he glimpsed Jim going through the door. He hesitated before going in and again once inside adjusting his eyes to the darkness and smoky haze. Jim was at a back table but rushed to meet him halfway. "Harry, good to see you. I didn't expect to beat you here." He grabbed Harry around the shoulders. "This isn't more bad news, is it?"

"Nothing like that." He waited until Jim sat down before continuing. "Actually, I want to talk to you about Mac Hudson."

"The cop who reopened Celeste's case?"

"Yeah. Were you aware Mac had a crush on Celeste in high school?"

Jim looked startled. "I didn't even know he went to school with my daughter. How did we miss that? What the hell? Don't forget, though, Celeste was the kind of girl who made a lot of friends."

"Let me put it this way because I felt stupid too, Jim. Remember Maximillan Hudson?"

"Oh my God, Maximillan is our Mac? Mac is that puppy dog that followed my daughter around?"

"Yep—one and the same."

"When did you put the pieces together?"

"Just last night after a conversation with him. I practically had to pull it out of him."

"What does all this mean?"

"Well, it might mean that Mac could have another agenda."

"Like what?"

"I haven't been able to put my finger on it yet."

"What are you saying?"

"I think it's odd that when all this started, he didn't mention he went to school with your daughter."

Jim glanced around the bar. "You know, now that you mention it, when Mac told Mike and me he was reopening Celeste's case, we thought there was something familiar about him, but that's as far as we went with it. Have you found out anything new?"

"Well, since we know Mac is Maximillan, we know he was in Celeste's class. Obviously, he's gone through quite a transformation since high school. We know he was an awkward kid back then and I imagine a lot of the teenagers made fun of him. Celeste probably took up for him, talked to him, maybe even chummed around with him on the school grounds. Who knows? I'm sure Mac resented Burton—probably jealous as hell."

"Celeste never dated Mac though. You're saying he was just a shadow?"

"Yes. As a matter of fact, I doubt Mac dated much in high school. Now, this brings me to what I want discuss with you."

"You have my interest."

"Good. After yesterday's meeting with him, I have an uneasy feeling that he is more invested in this case than I thought."

"Like how?"

"He got very agitated as we were talking. I don't know exactly how to put this, but something's not right."

"Are you telling me you suspect Mac Hudson was involved in Celeste's disappearance?"

Harry shook his head. "Frankly, I don't know what I'm saying. Mac's a damn good cop. If he was involved in Celeste's disappearance, I don't think he would reopen the case. My problem is—he's almost too motivated to find the guy that did it."

"Nothing wrong with that. I'm motivated too. Since he told us about investigating Celeste's disappearance again, I've tried to wipe the slate clean and start with fresh eyes although you know that's damn near impossible. If Mac's investigation turns up something bad happened to Celeste which, between you and me, I'm pretty sure of, I want to find the bastard that hurt my little girl and go from there."

"That's what we all want. Anyway, Jim, I wanted to pick your brain and see if you remembered anything about Mac or about Celeste's relationship with him."

"Wish I could come up with something. One thing about my girl, she felt sorry for the underdogs of the world. In fact, if we had kept all the stray animals she brought home, there wouldn't have been room for the rest of the family. So, if Mac was as different as we remember, I'm sure she would take him under her wing and try to make him feel better about himself and that would make him put her on a pedestal. Is that why he's so determined to find out what happened to her?"

"Maybe."

"Sorry I can't be more help, but now that you jogged my memory, I do remember him around the house. I'll still check with Mike. I'm going to see him now and I'll get back to you."

Michael fought constant drowsiness. If the doctors would stop medicating him, maybe he could make his way into the real world. He opened his eyes to see his dad coming through the door.

"Come in, dad, and don't worry about waking me up. I welcome any and all interruptions."

"Son, I need to discuss something with you. Up for it?"

"Absolutely. What's going on?"

After Jim explained his conversation with Harry, Michael hit the bed with his fist.

"Dad, finally a light bulb! I thought there was something familiar about Mac. I remember the guy now. Picture this…a skinny fifteen year old with large horn-rimmed glasses who looked like he might run if you talked to him. This probably sounds odd, but you know what comes back to me the most about the kid? His crazy clothes."

"Crazy?"

"You know, things that didn't match—plaid pants with striped shirts. He's come a long way, hasn't he?"

"Son, was he ever at the house?"

"Yeah, I think so."

"Well, if he was, I didn't pay much attention to him."

"Why is Harry so interested in Mac's relationship with Celeste?"

After Jim went over Harry's concerns, Michael agreed something was a little off. He also agreed the primary focus remained—find out what happened to Celeste. If it took Mac to do it, so be it.

Mac went along with Harry and waited a couple of days before checking in with Michael, but finally decided he couldn't put it off any longer. When he entered Michael's room, Rachel was giving him a back rub. Mac grinned broadly realizing this was the first time he had stretched his facial muscles in days.

"Boy, oh boy, does that look good!"

"Well, get in line."

Mac introduced himself to Rachel while shaking hands with Michael. "How are you and your son?"

"Better than a few days ago. Glad you could stop by—guess Harry got in touch with you."

"He did."

Michael maneuvered into the hospital gown before leaning back on the pillow. He pulled at the covers pointing to the gown. "These aren't the best looking but they work."

Mac nodded, waiting for him to settle.

"Mac, I've talked to Rachel about what you're doing—about reopening my sister's case. We've decided we don't want you to go any further."

"Michael…"

"We've made up our minds, Mac. Our family has been through enough—the shooting and my health scare has reinforced my decision to let the past go. There's no doubt my sister's disappearance just about killed my parents. Know what I mean?"

Mac moved toward the window before answering. "Of course, I know what you mean. Look, folks, I didn't reopen this on a whim. There's more going on here than your sister's disappearance."

"Like?"

"That's about all I can say."

Rachel walked to the other side of the bed. "Detective Hudson…"

"Make it Mac."

"Thanks. We want to cooperate and we certainly would like to lay Celeste's disappearance to rest, but does it have to be now? We have our hands full here and, honestly, I don't know how much more we can take."

"I understand, but as far as you're concerned, my investigation will be a matter of keeping you informed."

Michael's face reddened. "That's what I'm trying to tell you. The keeping us informed, as you put it, will hold our feet to the fire even more than they are now. It will be too much."

"Listen, Michael, your mother and dad have been through hell and I don't want to make it worse, but…" He stopped and looked at Rachel. "You probably saw something in the news about the Milford High girl."

Rachel nodded.

Michael drew in his breath. "Mac, you mentioned this girl to my dad and me in your office. Then I saw it come through the news wire."

"That's the one."

Michael twisted in the bed as Rachel moved to his side. "Honey, don't get upset."

"I'm okay, don't worry about me. The thought of something horrific happening to another young girl makes me sick."

"It makes all of us sick." Mac put his hand on Mike's shoulder. "Look, let's try this. I'll proceed as I'm doing now. I'll only contact you if and when it's absolutely necessary. In the meantime, you two take care of your family. How's that sound?"

Michael pulled himself upright in the bed. "C'mon, Mac. If we know you're going on with Celeste's investigation, how in God's name are we *not* going to think about it?" He turned toward Rachel. "What do you think, honey?"

"Mac, tell me a little bit about this Milford girl."

Mac looked down. "Rachel, the girl is, or was, a high school junior, a cheerleader, and between you and me, she might be in serious trouble or worse."

Rachel turned to Michael. "You may not want to hear this, but here goes. I've already said our family needs a break, but at the same time, my blood boils to think someone is out there doing God knows what to young girls. This might turn out to have nothing to do with your sister, Michael. Bottom line—I've changed my mind. I don't see how we can say no to Mac."

"You're right." He turned back to Mac. "Okay, Officer Mac Hudson, I'll call you after checking with dad."

"For whatever it's worth, I believe your dad will agree—it's the right decision." Mac paused and smiled. "Is it too soon to bring you up-to-date?"

Michael and Rachel laughed so hard, they cried. "We needed that."

"Mac, you're not laughing? Oh, Lord, you're serious."

"Yes, and what I'm about to tell you is very serious." Mac pulled two chairs by the bed. "There's a good chance that a crime scene was overlooked."

Michael sat upright. "What the hell are you talking about? Overlooked? Where?"

"Simmer down. Please, you must understand it was a long time ago. Police investigations were not as sophisticated in those days. They assumed your sister ran away—wrong—right—but nevertheless..."

"Sorry. You're right. I'll try to keep quiet."

"Okay. On a whim, I drove out to Concord—guess I wanted to take a walk down memory lane." He noticed Mike nodding. "Harry probably told you I was your sister's nerdy friend back then. Or, let me put it this way—she was one of the few kids who talked to me. Anyway, as I walked around Concord, I zoned out recalling high school years. The next thing I know I'm following this girl… don't ask… and I came face to face with a bulldozer. They're replacing the tennis courts and, get this—the old courts were built the year Celeste went missing. I stopped construction and declared it an active crime scene."

It took a while for the story to sink in before Rachel commented, "It's horrible and shocking, but stopping the construction was the right thing to do." She looked for Michael's approval.

"No question, it *was* the right thing to do, Mac. I hope you begin the investigation right away. You can count on dad's blessing."

Eleven

Bob tapped his pen on the desk pad. He scrawled Alex's name across his calendar. He couldn't put off talking to her any longer. As he buzzed her on the intercom—she walked in.

"Damn, Alex, we're on the same wave length."

He watched her move toward his desk hesitating just long enough for him to soak up her image—a vision in a purple sweater and skirt that clung to her like second skin.

"You like?"

Bob dropped his pen on the desk. "Not very professional of me, but, yeah, I like."

"You said the same wave length? I doubt it. You haven't called me about the hospital broadcast and that's all I'm thinking about."

He stood up and walked to the front of his desk. "Alex, there isn't going to be a hospital broadcast."

He expected a reaction and it didn't take long. He watched as her eyes flashed in harmony with redness that crept along her cheekbones.

"Why the hell not?"

"There are a lot of reasons—think about it and think about Michael."

Alex grinned. "I'm trying not to do that."

"Good for you. Anyway, it would be torturous for Michael to relive the horrible hours of not knowing whether his son was dead or alive."

"I know, but…"

"Hold on. Let me get this out and then you can have the floor. The news is saturated with the shooting and the aftermath. Besides that, Michael can hardly talk about any of this to his family or friends and he damn sure doesn't want to talk about it on radio."

Bob tried to ignore Alex's struggle to control her temper.

"It's Rachel, isn't it?"

"Yes and no. They're in agreement."

"Tell the truth, Bob. It's because it was my idea."

"Don't be ridiculous. Michael and Rachel need time to heal after almost losing their son. The other thing, it wouldn't be good for the families who lost children in this shooting."

"Okay, Bob. Think of it this way—Michael owes this to his public."

"How do you figure?"

"For one thing, the so-called miracle. What was that about?"

"Why do you say so-called?"

"How many miracles have you witnessed?" He shrugged. "That's my point, Bob. You and I aren't the most religious people, but don't you think the public deserves to know what happened to Michael's son—miracle or not."

"If you'll let me finish…"

She signaled him to go on.

"The decision-making committee discussed this from every angle. Bottom line—no broadcast. It's over, Alex—no more debate."

She stood, shut the door, and moved close to him.

"What are you doing?"

He felt her hands on his shoulders and her fingers trailing along his arms.

"Come on. This decision can't be final."

"As good as that feels, it won't work. Decision final—nothing will change it."

She stepped back. Her eyes hardened. "Now, you listen. If this is final, how's this for final? I quit…effective immediately. Replace me on the evening show and good luck with that!"

She stood close again and let her upper body rest against his chest before moving toward the door.

"Hold on, Alex, don't go off like that."

"Damn it all to hell. If this station doesn't have the balls to put on a simple broadcast that would do wonders for ratings, this isn't the place for a visionary like me. Plenty of stations would be kicked in the head to have me. Send my check ASAP." She started for the door but stopped. "Another thing, don't even think about suing me to finish out my contract. A court action would cost the station money and I know how the station hates to spend money." As she opened the door, she glanced over her shoulder. "By the way, tell Michael and Rachel to have happy lives in their small world."

"Alex..."

She slammed the door.

Bob called Michael. Alex's quick departure didn't make sense.

"Mike, I told Alex the hospital broadcast was axed."

"How did she take it?"

"She blew up and resigned. She's acting like a spoiled brat."

Michael agreed. "That's because she *is* a spoiled brat, Bob. You thought she acted weird when Celeste's calls started coming into the station. Didn't you tell me that you found her going through your mail one time?"

"Yeah, she was in my office. I didn't know what the hell she was doing there and I still don't know."

Michael's voice sounded edgy. "I don't know. Damn strange. She had a great job on the upswing and walking out because of not getting her way, stupid. Something else. The Concord story will stay hot for a while—the Milford High story is heating up too. Alex had plenty of juicy stories to sharpen her claws on. She's just throwing a bitch fit. She'll be back."

Bob stared into space. "Don't think so. If the station sues, she'll get a good lawyer to fight them and she'll get out of her contract. I think we've seen the last of Alex."

"I have to cut this short, buddy. The doc is here. I'm going to twist his arm to release me tomorrow. Talk to you later."

Bob had a couple of hours before the evening broadcast. He headed to the hospital to check on Mike's release.

He opened the door to Rachel and Jim Adams' laughter. "Now, that's what I like to hear. We've had enough doom and gloom to last a lifetime."

Jim got up and shook hands with Bob.

"You can say that again. I hate to cut out as soon as you get here, Bob, but I want to check on Chris."

Bob watched Jim close the door. "Your dad is a strong man, isn't he?"

"One of the strongest I know."

"So, did the doc spring you?"

"He did, as a matter of fact. I'm escaping in the morning."

"Guess one more night won't kill you."

Rachel grimaced. "Don't say that, Bob. I'd like to have him home with me right now."

Michael threw her a kiss before turning back to Bob. "Anything new on Alex?"

"No, but it's only been a couple of hours. Give her time. I expect to see her at the news desk tonight screaming at the guy I called in."

"Who's taking over?"

"I put Bill in for the night. If Alex is still AWOL, I'll go over the roster tomorrow."

The head nurse knocked and came in apologizing for the interruption. She had discharge directions for Mike and Rachel, but motioned Bob to keep his seat. Once she left, Michael looked at Bob. "Buddy, *there's* a woman for you."

"Nurse Abigail?"

"Her name is not Abigail, but, yeah, I've seen her give you the eye several times."

Bob chuckled. "Man, if a woman gave me the eye and I missed it, I am getting old…hold it, I mean older."

"I'm serious, man. You haven't noticed her before?"

"I've seen her around, but haven't paid much attention to her."

Michael grinned. "Listen to this guy, Rach. He hasn't noticed her. Get out of here, man. Now, listen. All I'm saying—instead of walking around like a heartsick puppy fantasizing about Alex, pick someone more your style."

"Someone my style? I don't know if you're insulting me or not."

"No, no. I've told you before—Alex is too young for you. She's looking for a good time—you're looking for a partner."

Bob moved close to Rachel and put his arm around her. "I tell you, *Mister* Michael Adams, *this* woman is what I'd like—not Nurse Abigail."

Rachel patted his cheek. "Bob, in all seriousness, I think the nurse in question could be interested in you. She's very attractive. I've seen her looking you over, but hey, forget about her. Look for someone like me, although I doubt you'll find her. I'm one of a kind, you know."

Bob kissed Rachel on the forehead. "You can say that again, good lookin', but you belong to my best buddy." He moved to the other side of the bed. "Okay, Mike, since you're getting out of this joint tomorrow, I'll stroll out to the nurses' station and see if I can find Nurse Abigail." He turned before closing the door. "Thanks for caring about me, you two. I'll touch base in the morning."

Rachel drove to the hospital excited and relieved her man was finally coming home. The world would be perfect if Chris was coming too, but his healing was slower. The only bright spot—his friends were giving him a lot of attention and he loved it.

On the other hand, Michael was like a caged animal. She stepped into his room to find him dressed and pacing.

"God, Rach, I thought you'd never get here."

"Calm down, honey. I'm a half hour early."

"I know, I know. Sorry. I'll be glad to get out of here whenever I can."

About that time, the nurse entered with a stack of papers

to sign. As Mike finished the last page, Harry and Joan came through the door.

"What the hell are you two doing here?"

"Bob told us you were getting sprung. We're here to fight off your adoring public."

"Man, there's not going to be any..."

"Look out the window."

Michael was surprised to see the press lined up.

"Don't worry, buddy, we have it covered."

The nurse guided the wheelchair toward Michael.

"No way I'm getting into that thing."

"Oh, yes you are, Mr. Adams, or you're not leaving here."

He lowered himself into the chair. "Okay. If this is what it takes, let's boogie."

Rachel took Michael's arm as they climbed the steps to their home's second floor. "Honey, I'm fine. I'm probably in better shape than I've been in a while with all the rest. In fact, too much rest."

"Make me happy. Lay down for a bit and then we'll have lunch—maybe in bed. How does that sound?"

"Yes, dear." He took her hand and pulled her into bed with him.

"Michael, behave. You're not up for that yet."

He chuckled. "I think I am."

Rachel hugged him. They held each for a few minutes soaking up each other's comfort.

"You know, Rach, I have to admit you're right. Guess I'm kinda tired after all."

"Thought so." She got up, kissed him on the cheek, and pulled the shades. "I'll check on you in a bit, honey."

As Rachel walked past the library on her way to the kitchen for some hot tea, she noticed the boxes she had retrieved from storage. She was exhausted, but something drew her to the library. She stood looking at the boxes—it was time.

As she touched one, she swallowed hard, refusing to cry.

Once the lid was off, she couldn't turn back. All her childhood memories would tumble out like Pandora's box, but her memories were nothing like the horrible tribulations Pandora released. Her remembrances were of love, happiness, and wondrous times spent with her mother. Tears filled her eyes—her heart was still raw after all these years.

She looked at her mother's picture and ran her fingers along her beautiful image. "My husband and son almost died, mom. I can't believe I'm saying almost died—a nightmare. Now I finally know what you meant when you were so sick and told me not to waste my prayers and promises on you, to save them for someone more important. Mom, you were all I had. I didn't want to let you go. You said you wanted me to enjoy your legacy, the wealth and fame you gained as Margaret Benson, photographer, but all I wanted was you. I made God so many promises if He'd let you live."

Rachel pulled her hair back, twisted it, and secured it with a rubber band. Time to get to work. She thought about the discussions she had with her mother about auctioning off some of her photographs. They wanted to raise money for a wing at the children's hospital. They had even begun plans when her mother took ill. She promised she would carry out their plans, but after her mom died, she didn't have the heart to go on with it.

Rachel stood to stretch and looked at herself in the mirror over the fireplace. Her mother's eyes looked back at her. She continued to stare, wondering how she could get so wrapped up in herself, how she could be so selfish? She whispered, "Mom, did it take almost losing my son and husband to open the part of my soul filled with your essence?" She rested her head in her arms on the mantle, took a deep breath, and embraced her mother's love and joy for life. All the sweet memories flowed into her heart like warm honey.

A voice interrupted. "Rachel, hey Rach."

Startled, Rachel turned to see Father Andrew. She struggled to return to the present. "Damn, I mean gee, I must have lost track of time. I didn't hear the bell." She stepped back, almost falling over one of the boxes. "Oh, hell!" Father Andrew caught her before she hit the floor. He pulled her to her feet and wrapped her in a bear hug, looking very serious. She scanned his handsome face, square jaw, unruly dark hair, and that sexy little cleft in his chin—a younger version of Harry.

He spoke first. "Such language in front of a servant of God."

She tried to appear ashamed but how could she when the beginning of a smile appeared in his green eyes. They burst out laughing as he released her.

"I hope you don't mind I let myself in. You didn't answer the bell. The door was unlocked by the way. Not a good idea. When I glanced through the window, you seemed so troubled."

"Don't apologize. Believe me, I can't think of a better surprise at this very moment." A tear started its way down her cheek. She traced its tracks with her fingers. "Sorry, I seem to have a lot of tears lately."

"Rachel, I know this has been tough time for you, but your boys are still with us. If my source was correct, you have one of them home. Thank God."

She hugged him again. "You're right and I've been remembering how blessed I am."

"So, what's with all these boxes? Don't tell me you're moving."

"No, no, quite the contrary. I'm digging into my past and realize it's time to pay a debt that's long overdue."

Rachel knew Andrew was waiting for an explanation, but she just wasn't up for it now. She saw him glancing at photographs on the desk.

"You can pick them up."

She waited for his reaction.

"Rachel, these are absolutely beautiful. I was going to ask who took these, but I see your mother's name in the corner. Margaret Benson—awe inspiring work." He went through the stack of magazine covers—Benson's name inscribed at the bottom of each. "I'd forgotten your mother's considerable fame."

"Yes, her photos were in high demand."

"Hey, check out this box. Your name is on it with a message. It has to be special. Do you mind if I read it?"

"Of course not. Read it aloud."

"It says, 'Rachel, my dear, dear daughter. These photographs have always brought me solace. Let them comfort you. All my love, Mom.'"

Rachel fought tears once again.

Andrew put his arm around her shoulder. "Come on now, don't be sad. Your mother gave you a special gift. If you're up for it, let's spread these on the floor and go through them together." He took her chin in his hand. "I don't want to intrude. If you'd rather be alone, I'll get out of here, but I'd love to spend some time with you..."

"Say no more. Stay, Father."

"Drop the Father stuff. You're like a sister to me and Harry."

Rachel raised an eyebrow.

"No, not the kind that wears a habit."

"Bless you, Andrew, you could always make me smile. As a matter of fact, I could really use the help, as well as the company."

"Okay, then, back to this special gift box. Look at these pyramids. Man, I didn't realize you two got around like this. I have to tell you, Rach, this kind of work shouldn't be buried in boxes. They're part of your past, your heritage."

"You're right, and that reminds me of something I was thinking about when you came in. Before my mother died, we talked about auctioning off some of her photographs to raise money for a new hospital wing. She felt guilty about making money on something she loved doing so much and she wanted to give something back. So, why don't you give me a hand choosing some photos to auction?"

"Sounds good—a lovely way to spend time with a dear friend. I only have one question."

"That is?"

"How do we choose when they're all so good?"

"You're right, but I can use your saintly, Irish eyes to help."

Andrew looked away. "These eyes have seen some pretty sad images lately. It will be nice to look at beautiful ones for a while—you and the pictures."

"Andy, you were always so sweet and sexy—still are." She could feel her face warm. "Guess I need to go to confession now telling a priest he's sexy. So many of my girlfriends were disappointed when you took your vows."

He answered in his best Irish brogue, "Go on with you, girl."

Rachel laughed. It felt good. "Okay, you start looking at the photos and I'll get some coffee and cookies. How's that sound?"

"You have to ask?"

Rachel hurried to the kitchen thankful for Andrew's visit. If she ever needed a friend, today was the day. When she returned to the library, tray of cookies in hand, Andrew was still rummaging through a box. She put the tray in front of him and watched as he grabbed a cookie and stuffed it in his mouth.

"You guys are all the same."

"Don't let this collar fool you, lovely lady, a cookie monster lurks beneath."

As they settled down, cups in hand, Rachel noticed some pictures Andrew had put aside.

He handed her a magnifying glass. "Look at a few of these. I can't believe what I'm seeing, but I have to ask, just what *am* I seeing?"

She studied the pictures through the glass. Her hand trembled as she sunk to the floor. "Oh my."

"Are you okay, Rachel?"

"Yes. I'd forgotten all about these. I recall my mother couldn't get over the fact that we were there to witness this miraculous happening. She said it was a blessing from God for her to capture this image with her camera. I was so young; I had no clue. I don't think I ever really believed."

"You're not making any sense. You didn't believe what?"

"Sorry, Father—I mean Andy. I was with mother when these

were taken. We were in Egypt." She turned the photograph over. "See, April, 1968, Coptic Church, Zeitoun, Egypt."

He rubbed the back of his neck. "Zeitoun strikes a chord. Dear God, you *did* say Zeitoun, Egypt, didn't you?"

"I did, yes."

"Are these the real thing?"

"Yes. If you look at the back again, you'll recognize my mother's handwriting."

"Well, I am totally blown away. I heard about this, of course, but honestly—I didn't know what to think about it." He turned the photograph over and over. "So, you and your mom were actually there in 1968. I'll be damned."

"Andy! Now we both need to go to confession."

"These are fascinating, Rachel. I'm totally lost in them."

"You saw mom's note—these were her favorites."

"She gave them to you for comfort. I would say opening this box today is perfect timing."

"Yes, there couldn't be a better time. What do they say? God works in mysterious ways."

"Are you saying that finding these pictures today is a mystery to you?"

"Actually, the more I think about it, the answer is no. It reminds me of the tapestries the nuns used to make—every stitch, every thread, filled in a picture and the threads continually made the picture more interesting. Going through my mother's work has helped fill in the picture of my life's tapestry."

TWELVE

Mac shuffled the stack of files around on his desk. The more he worked on the Celeste Adams' case, the more convoluted it became. He moved to the door motioning to one of the men outside.

"Harry in yet?"

"Yeah, I'm headed that way—I'll get him for you."

"Don't bother. I'll find him."

Mac walked into Harry's office without knocking. "Hey man, how are you this beautiful fall morning?"

"Cold as hell, but I kinda like it. What's going on?"

"I want to go over some things with you."

"What's on your mind? Silly question."

"Right."

Harry grinned with a sideways twist to his lips. "I'm pretty much up on everything, but…"

Mac pointed his index fingers at him, simulating guns. "Seriously, if you have time, come back to my office. I'd like to look at the persons of interest again, at least the ones we have so far, and see if anything jumps out at us."

Back in Mac's office, he pointed to the corkboard. "I've gone through these files and looked at that board so many times I'm cross-eyed. I still come up with Burton. It looks like we're on the right track." He thumped Burton's card on the board with his knuckles. "There's no telling what this S.O.B.'s been involved in."

"I agree—at least for the time being. What about these other names?"

"Exactly what I want to talk to you about. Don't get me wrong—I'd like nothing better than to close the case on Burton today, but let's face it—we don't have enough. He's clever and he's covered his tracks, but guys like this slip up eventually."

"Not every time."

"Yeah, but if we're right and he's our man, we have to get him before he gets by with it again."

"Again? Come on, Mac. It's been twenty-eight years since Celeste disappeared. You can't think Burton's involved in the Milford incident." Harry scanned the chronological list.

"I'm saying that and more. The only good thing about the Milford case—it's fresh and away from Concord. If it is Burton, the new technology will be his undoing. There's more. You'll see I've added some names on the board." Waiting for Harry's nod, he went on. "As much as I'm sure Burton is our man, I won't be accused of heading up a lynch mob. When I went through the file, I made notations on everyone who was connected to Celeste in *any* way. This includes her family, the priest and nuns at her church, the principal at Concord, her teachers, her friends, and her friends' families."

"You're thorough—I give you that."

Mac grinned. "Got that right. Now, I mentioned her family—they were cleared back when all this came down."

"I should hope so."

"You know we look at family first and even Gil got that one right. Okay, follow the list there."

"McCoy, the principal, why?"

"The *why* for him and the teachers is because they saw Celeste every day—at least the teachers did. I don't recall her ever getting out of line much and having to go see old McCoy."

Harry sat on the corner of Mac's desk remembering the look on Mac's face at Indigo's. "I guess you would know that."

"Damn it, there you go again. I don't need sarcasm. I'm not trying to pin anything on Burton without just cause, but I do want to find out what happened to Celeste."

"What about Gil's theory that she ran away?"

Mac grinned and shook his head. "You know her family. You know how she was raised. She loved them too much to hurt them that way."

Harry's face saddened. "How did you feel about Celeste dating Burton?"

Mac wheeled around aggressively as Harry ducked. "Are you saying what I think you're saying?"

"No, I'm not. What I'm saying, are the feelings you had for Celeste back in the day coloring your attitude toward Burton now?"

"Maybe at the beginning, but I'm past that now. I wouldn't be much of a lawman if I let that happen, would I?"

"Okay, Mac, any other names get your juices running?"

"Yeah, the cheerleader squad leader and the list of cheerleaders."

"And the reason?"

Mac chuckled. "Well, you know how some women are—the green eyed monster. Look at it this way. Celeste was a pretty girl and Burton liked her. The rest of the girls probably wanted him to like them too. When this investigation began, no one thought about the other girls on the squad or the teacher in charge…"

"Things have changed over the last twenty years."

"Sadly for the worst. You've been in this crazy business of ours far too long not to realize that anything is possible. Don't forget how popular Burton was in those days. All the girls tried to catch his eye. Celeste was one of them and she *did* catch his eye. You don't think that would have made some of the girls envious?"

"Guess so, but enough to do away with her? I'm not convinced."

"I didn't expect you to be." Mac met his gaze. "I'm just saying that I'm checking everyone out again and that brings me to Celeste's best girlfriend at the time."

"It's been too long. Who was that?"

"Tracy Fritz. The snapshot I put up is the only one I've been able to find."

Harry studied the picture. "The old guy in the picture—that's her father, isn't it?"

"I think so. He looks pretty worn out."

Harry put on his glasses. "Another set of eyes helps, right? I recognize the old man now, but it's been a lot of years. Anyway, I think he's still around. Great job, Mac. You're melting away the years. Exactly what I need—a clear picture of the past."

"Okay, to refresh your memory even more. Tracy was on Concord's cheerleading squad—that's about all her father allowed her to do. Her family owned a farm and according to Mr. Fritz, his wife left when the girl was starting high school. This meant Tracy had to help out around the place and couldn't participate in much at school. She probably had it pretty rough after her mother left and guess her old man thought allowing her to be a cheerleader was the least he could do."

Mac flipped through his post-its in the file until he came to the one marked Tracy. "Here's a note on this from one of the investigating officers. Damn, nothing more than what I told you. The only notation is 'Celeste's best friend'."

"You don't suspect her, do you?"

"No, but I'd like to talk to her. Young girls share secrets and maybe they shared a secret about Burton or someone else. Harry, look at this list of Celeste's activities during the year she disappeared—specifically those connected to our man, Burton."

Mac stared at Harry's face. "You're frowning. Why?"

"I don't see a lot of relevance in these other people."

"Relevance?"

"Well, connection—you know what I mean."

Mac sat in his chair and rubbed the back of his neck, a frequent habit these days. "Harry, don't quote me to anyone, and I mean anyone, but I don't think Gil did the best investigative job here."

"Mac—"

"Let me finish. I've quarreled with myself whether I should mention this or not, but you were involved at the time…"

"A rookie."

"I know. In my rookie days, I was afraid to approach a senior detective on the job. My M.O. was to shut up and learn."

"Mac, maybe Gil did less than a stellar job here, but he was a good cop."

"I know, I just think he got a little sloppy. That's all."

Harry moved to one of the chairs across from Mac, and leaned his elbows on the desk. "Guess I'm taking this personal, but you're right, Gil might have been a little sloppy, but let's give the old guy a break."

Mac continued to peruse the cards on his bulletin board ending up on Burton's. The man could creep into the darkest crevices of his mind.

John and Ed came in the office about that time. "Want to see us?"

Harry and Mac gave them the high sign before Mac started. "Yeah, I was looking for you a couple of hours ago, but since you're two of the best cops on the force, I'll overlook it." Mac winked at Harry. "I got these two guys involved, young and not tainted by old ties." He turned to Ed.

"Harry and I were just talking about Tracy Fritz, Celeste Adams' best girlfriend in high school and her dad, Ralph. According to the file, when Celeste disappeared, old Ralph seemed concerned about his daughter's closeness to Celeste. Don't get me wrong—looks like he didn't object to his daughter having a friend, but you probably recall the notation that he eavesdropped on the girls one time—probably did it more than once. Who knows? He was probably afraid Tracy would get some ideas, you know boy ideas, from Celeste and he didn't like it."

"Healthy for fifteen year olds, wouldn't you say?"

Ed smiled. "When I was fifteen, I would agree with you, but I imagine from a father's standpoint, my view would be different."

John walked toward the window. "Mac, read on. What else is in the file?"

"Just that Tracy left for a better life and her dad said he couldn't blame her. After his wife was gone, it was just the two of them.

He needed her help to run the farm—a tough life."

"Harry, you were at that interview with Gil. Was Fritz angry?"

"I've been sitting here thinking back. I recall driving out to the farm with Gil and being surprised how old and haggard Tracy's father looked. He didn't seem angry, just sad. Sad, lonely and old before his time. I *will* say he impressed me as being on the level. As far as connecting any of our persons of interest to the new Milford High situation, it's been a long time since Celeste and Tracy went off our radar. It's unusual for a killer to wait this long before killing again..." he hesitated, "yet, we've seen cases in recent years that go the other way, Mac."

"You're right. Now, men, stay with me here—before any of you bring this up, I don't know any possible motive these people on Celeste Adams' suspect board would have to harm the Milford High girl. For that matter, I don't know what motive they would have had to get rid of Celeste either." Mac clicked his tongue several times. "You know what they say though—who knows what lurks in the minds of men."

Ed spoke up, "Don't you mean hearts of men?"

"Yeah, same difference."

Harry grinned. "Okay, there *is* one person on the board who could have a motive to get rid of Celeste and we all know who that is—your favorite suspect, Mr. Ted Burton."

Mac rolled his head in a clockwise motion before moving to the board. "Let's talk about Teddy boy again."

John spoke up. "I know you don't want to hear this, but I still say he's a lover not a killer. His background is a little shady..."

"Shady? C'mon, John." Mac punched the card with his fist. "I think he's a shithead and capable of anything—murder included. Men, check on the progress of the Hornsby/Milford case and see if you can dig up anything, I mean *anything*, on Burton's connection to Pamela Hornsby. Keep me in the loop."

Mac reviewed his To Do list—a helpful tool in law school. He sifted through the checked off items:

Touch base with Chief regarding status of Adams' case.

Construction agreement to halt demolition of Concord's tennis courts and
Designate area as an active crime scene.
Get in touch with Bill Blake, H&M supervisor.
Contact Dr. Lillian Katz, forensic anthropologist.

Then he called Harry to clear his deck for the afternoon before driving to Concord to continue their journey—why and how Celeste Adams disappeared.

⤧◎◉⤦

When Mac and Harry arrived, Mac pointed to Bill and Lillian marking off a large square. The two were so intent on their discussion—they didn't see them approaching.

"Bill, good to see you…" Mac paused to look at Lillian, "and you are the good doctor?"

Before Lillian could answer, Harry took a step toward her. "Lillian Katz! Remember me?"

She smiled broadly. "How could I ever forget you, Harry O'Donnell?"

Mac observed their exchange. There was definitely something going on between them. For some unknown reason, he felt a twinge of jealousy. How could that be? He had never seen this woman before. He had spoken with Lillian several times on the phone but hadn't known what to expect in the looks department. He was more than pleasantly surprised. Her striking grey eyes were the first thing he noticed—they were filled with compassion. She appeared to be close to his age, short-cropped black hair that would look butch on most women, but with her delicate features, the style looked very feminine. It also looked like she enjoyed working out as much as he did—maybe more. He was shocked she got his testosterone going.

He knew from their phone conversations he could work with this woman. She was direct and to the point.

Harry touched her elbow. "Lillian, it's been too long. We'll have to play catch up once we get all this behind us."

"I'd love that. Give me a call." She turned toward Mac and Bill. "Sorry, gentlemen. Bill, before you begin, I'd like to confirm to Mac…" she paused looking at Harry. "Are you on this case too, Harry?"

"Looks like it. You'll get tired seeing us, Lillian."

"Not a chance. Who's lead or is this a double-header?"

Harry grinned. "Well, it's definitely a team effort, but Mac is stuck with most of the paperwork."

"Good enough. Bill, take over—then I'll explain my part."

Mac didn't miss Bill watching them with interest—sizing them up. He couldn't blame him—he and Harry were probably a different combination of cops. Mac knew he could count on Bill, a sturdy 5'10" man who looked like he could take care of himself in a fair fight.

Mac responded. "Ball's in your court, Bill."

"Okay, here goes. I believe you have all worked with H&H in the past in one capacity or another, but it won't hurt to go over a few things. Our equipment will be here in the morning and by that time I, along with Lillian, will have marked off our initial exploration area. Lillian, that okay with you?"

"Of course, Bill, usual procedure."

"Mac, you've covered necessary notices and paperwork with the school and everyone else involved, right?"

"Done."

"Okay, then. All that's left for me to say is I will contact Mac when and if something is found. How does that sound?"

They all nodded agreement.

Bill took over again. "One more thing. I know you hate to hear this is painstakingly slow work, but it is. However, that said, we'll do our best to move it along as fast as we can. Now, back to Lillian. She has some good news for you fellows."

Lillian's smile fractured the seriousness of her face. "I do have. It'll make your day."

"We can use some good news," Harry said. "We've had enough bad to last a lifetime."

"The coroner has given his okay to set up a temporary lab on-site."

"Can't believe that. What's the catch?"

"Wish I could answer that. All I know is I received notification that a mobile lab would be dispatched to Concord tomorrow. Someone's pulling strings."

Mac grinned. "I for one am not going to question it. Harry?"

"Not me. What else, Lillian?"

"As Bill said, this is slow work, so don't expect too much too soon. In fact, we may find nothing. From what you told me, Mac, this investigation is based on supposition more than anything else at this point. Is that right?"

"Yes and no. You're looking at a cop there—don't get embarrassed, Harry, who has been around the block a time or two. His investigative skills top the ranks. I'm not too bad with these situations either. Our instincts tell us we may find what happened to a young girl who disappeared 28 years ago. We know both of you will do a good job. Find us something!"

Mac and Harry drove to Concord the next morning. Mac's excitement transferred to his partner. "Harry, I can't believe my eyes. Look at what they've accomplished." Not waiting for a reply, he took off toward Bill.

"Hey, man, did you start at five o'clock?"

"Actually we got the equipment out at four."

"That early?"

"We had special permission for noise, but by the time everything was in place, it wasn't that early. Anyway, Lillian and I stayed last night to be sure the area was marked off the way we wanted it. My men are used to this work, Mac, and they know I want everything done pronto. No need to go into details here—you can see what we're doing."

"Where's Lillian?"

He pointed to one of the far corners. "She's over there. That woman's a whiz."

Harry grinned. "I can vouch for that."

About that time, a whistle pierced the silence.

"What in the hell was that?"

Bill chuckled. "A signal. Lillian wants us over there. Come on, guys."

Lillian waved. "Where you two been? Bill and I saw the sun come up."

"That's what we hear." Mac scanned the area. "Looks to me like you got the gang going too."

Bill slapped a glove against Harry's arm. "You two want to help? We can use more hands."

"Out of our league, Bill, but we'll hang around for a while. How long will it take to clear the first area?"

"Lillian, I told you these guys would want everything like yesterday." He looked at Mac. "It won't take long for the first pass, but that's just the beginning. Cool your heels and go about your other business." Bill smiled. "You do have other business, don't you?"

Mac threw up his hands. "You got me. We'll be back later and, Lillian, I expect to see you down in the dirt finding something."

As Mac and Harry made their way to the car, Mac quizzed Harry. "Hey, man, what's with you and Lillian Katz?"

Harry winked. "I was wondering how long it would take you to go there."

"So, give it up."

"Nothing to tell. I met Lil at a forensic seminar right after I became a cop. We connected, dated on and off—more off than on. I never followed up on it and that's that. Case closed."

They stopped at the bleachers.

"Harry, I wish I could go through my high school years again looking and knowing what I do now."

"I don't know, Mac. I wouldn't want to go through all that reading and testing again."

"Same here—take it back."

As soon as they got back to the station, Harry went his own way to transfer papers to the Chief on the case he had been working on. He was glad to unload it—political drama. He also wanted to call Joan out of Mac's earshot.

Seeing Lillian Katz brought back memories of lost time. Joan was the only one who could soothe some of his regrets. "Hey, Joan. What time are you off duty?"

"Harry, hello to you too. I should be off by six. I'm working north of the city the rest of the day but should be back by five. What's on your mind?"

"You mostly."

"Those are words I like to hear. What else?"

"If you don't have plans for dinner, why don't we get together about seven? We can go out if you like or..."

"How about coming to my place? We can relax."

"I'll bring wine."

"I've had you on my mind all morning. What's going on?"

"Nothing and everything—doesn't make sense, does it? You say I've been on your mind—that's a good thing."

"It always is. Harry, I always know when something is happening with you. Want to talk over the phone?"

"No, no, and definitely no. I'll be at your place about seven."

Joan opened her door to a refreshed Harry O'Donnell. A rust colored shirt topped off pressed jeans. He didn't miss her look of approval.

"Officer Roberts, you take my breath away."

"May I say the same for you, Harry. Come inside before my neighbors get an eye full."

Harry wrapped her in his arms and held on tightly. Joan pushed him back a bit. "Okay, what's going on? Have you had bad news?"

He led her to the kitchen. "Tell you what. I'll get the scotch—scotch and water, okay with you?"

"You know it is."

Harry looked amused. "You know, Joanie, you're the only woman I know who drinks scotch."

"You telling me it's a man's drink?"

"Well," Harry drawled, "maybe, but there's nothing manly about you, honey. Anyway, grab some glasses."

"Harry, I barely had time to change clothes before you came. So..."

"No dinner, right?"

"Sorry." She held up her index finger. "But, snacks to the rescue. I've got tons of stuff if you're up for that."

"Not hungry, thanks."

Harry put his arm around her shoulders. "Want to sit on the patio?" He waited for her nod before guiding her toward the terrace loveseat. He took her glass along with his, put them on the small side table, and pulled her close. His lips melted into hers with a long, passionate kiss.

She smiled. "Okay, now I know something is up." She handed him his drink. "Is it the station?"

"Before I get into that, there are some things I want to talk to you about."

Joan curled up beside him, folding her legs under her. She laid her head on his shoulder. "I'm all yours."

"You know, I don't tell you enough how beautiful you are..."

"Stop it and tell me what's bothering you."

"*You* are what's bothering me at the moment." He put his finger across her lips. "Be quiet and let me have my say. You are a magnificent woman in every way, Joan, with the loveliest eyes I have ever seen."

"You are so full of it."

"Most women would love to hear this."

"I'm not most women. Have you forgotten I'm a cop first and a woman second?"

"That's what I want to talk about."

"I don't understand."

"You might if you would close your lovely lips. Now, I ran into an old friend this morning..."

"Male, female?"

"As a matter of fact, female, but it only got me thinking about the years you and I have been together. They have been great, Joan…"

"Hold it right there, buster. Are you dumping me?"

"God, no. Drink your scotch and give me some time, will ya? You know we talked at one time about marriage. We decided our jobs didn't fit matrimony."

"I know all that," Joan countered. "I think we were right, don't you?"

"That's what I want to ask you. Do you still think we were right? Do you still think we couldn't make it work?"

"Is this a proposal?"

"No…just something to think about, you know."

She unfolded her legs, stood, and moved toward the kitchen. "I can see this conversation calls for more strong stuff."

"You bet."

Harry couldn't take his eyes off her as she moved around the kitchen. "You don't look like a cop tonight, Joanie."

"No?"

"No. If I didn't know you and had to guess, I'd say an actress or dancer—never a cop."

"Well, that's what I am through and through." She took his hand leading him back to the patio. She cuddled close again. "Okay, dear Harry, go on."

"Guess I'm feeling melancholy and getting older. It makes you stop and think. We have a wonderful relationship, Joanie. Frankly, my life would be empty without you."

"Oh, come on, you're going too far. Your life is so full, you don't have time for anything else."

"That's not true. The shooting at Concord, what Mike and his family have gone through—not to mention the other families—has made me aware of how short life is."

"Our work makes us aware of that every day. We're continually reminded about humanity's strengths and weaknesses. You're just feeling low tonight and I think I know why. You're on the Celeste's Adams' cold case, aren't you?"

"Correct. Mac and I are the lead investigators." Harry sighed and finished his drink. "I need you tonight and something else."

"What?"

"We should rethink the marriage thing. Shhhh, before you say anything, I'm not talking now."

"You're talking when grey hair takes over?" Joan laughed.

He pulled her close kissing her hard. "It's not funny, Joan. I'm serious here and you're stepping on my manly pride."

Joan looked deep into his eyes embracing his face with her hands. "Never, I repeat, never would I want to do that. You know I love you. I fell in love with you the first time I worked with you. Harry, I know you. We are old souls and the work we do is ingrained on them. I truly believe we were born to make a difference in this world. I don't know if it's a blessing or a curse." She took his hand. "I can't imagine not having you in my life. So, if your putting a proposal on the table, I say we should consider it. But for now, let the rest of the night take care of itself."

THIRTEEN

Mac received a call from Bill Blake. They needed him and Harry at the site as soon as possible.

When they arrived, Bill motioned them to the side grid area. Lillian was bent over sifting material. She mumbled she'd be with them in a minute.

"You are a sight, woman."

She stood and put her hand up. "Help me out of here, guys." She twirled around to look at Mac. "Listen, you, I'd like to see you get down in the dirt and come up clean."

"Oops, didn't mean to step on toes. I should say, you look like a hard working anthropologist. Is that better?"

"You two, stop it," Bill interrupted. "We've got some news for you and Harry."

"What you got?"

"Tell them, Lillian."

"We found partials of what looks like human finger bones. I transported them to the lab. Now, I was looking at some other things…"

"What?"

"Hold on, Mac. Harry, get him under control, would you?" She smiled at Mac. "Just kidding. I know how serious this is, but you have to lighten up a little."

She called to her assistant, "Mark, say hello to Mac and Harry. You'll be seeing a lot of them. Okay, photograph and bag what we found. Take the material to the lab so they can see it."

"Lillian, what exactly did you find?" Harry responded.

Bill spoke up. "Junk—at least that's what it looks like to me."

"What's junk to some is treasure to others, Bill. In a case like this, everything could be important."

Harry knelt. "From what I can tell, that stuff looks like jewelry pieces."

"That's what it is. Looks like chains and charms of some kind—maybe off bracelets or necklaces. It's hard to tell until we get them cleaned up. There was something else too, a girl's purse. I've already taken it to the lab."

"What kind of purse—something a younger girl or woman would carry?"

"Yes, but purses are kinda generic. You know, the type of purse and age of carrier isn't determined by size. It's a small, cloth type bag with a shoulder strap."

"Man, this was quick, don't you think?"

"Yes, Mac, and because of finding these things, Bill is going deeper in this particular area in the morning. We're still working the 3 foot level out from this point today." She turned to Bill. "I need to talk to these guys about the entomologist. Be back in a few. "Men, follow me to the lab and I'll show you the findings."

"What or who the hell are you talking about, Lillian? A ento...what?"

Harry laughed. "If you had gone to the forensic seminar with Lillian and me, you'd know."

"So, I didn't. Explain."

"He's a bug expert—sort of like 'The Orkin Man.'"

"He would do what?"

"He would ascertain how long the remains have been in the ground. I'd recommend Dr. Bruce Williamson. He's in this area and he's top notch. If you approve, I'll get in touch with him."

"Would the next five minutes be too soon?"

Lillian chuckled. "I'll see what I can do. Mac, you gave me a preliminary rundown on your case, so I hope we find enough skeletal remains to give us clues regarding sex, height, weight, and age of the victim. We should also be able to tell if there's been damage to the skeleton—knife marks, fractures, etc."

Mac smiled. "You're going to give us all that?"

"*If*, and that's a big if, we find sufficient remains. It all depends on what we find. I'll give you what I can."

"I know, Lillian—just giving you a hard time."

Mac looked around the mobile lab as he listened to Lillian urging him and Harry to relax for a few minutes—grab coffee if they wanted. He watched her open a pull-out table and covered it with sterile cloths.

"Gentlemen, before we start, you are both seasoned policemen and have been through this before, but I still have to remind you not to touch anything. The remains we find must stay sterile for my tests. So, again, don't touch anything—even with gloves."

She laid the bones on the table. Then, she put the jewelry findings on a separate table commenting they had to be cleaned.

"Gentlemen, our exploration begins."

Mac held his breath and rested his hand on Harry's back. He knew, and he was well aware that Harry did as well, there was a chance the remains of someone very dear to them could be on the tables.

Mac exhaled loud enough for Lillian and Harry to glance his way.

Lillian continued, "Let's begin with the bones. I want to point out that it's particularly curious that a few stones appear to be embedded in several of the finger bones. For this to happen, one would have to use extreme pressure—"

"Extreme pressure? What from—the weight of the soil and concrete?"

"No, Mac. What I'm trying to say, and not doing a very good job of it, it's very possible that the small stones could have been shoved into the skin so hard and pressure kept there so long that the objects became one with the bone." She leaned forward. "Take a look on this other table. All the jewelry pieces need cleaning, but you can recognize the objects. Anything look familiar to either of you?"

Mac and Harry spoke at the same time. "Lillian..."

"One at a time, gentlemen. You first, Mac."

"Nothing looks familiar. How about you, Harry?"

Harry struggled to get words out. "Can't be sure." He kept staring at the stones embedded in the finger bones.

Mac noted Harry's hesitation. "Take your time. Is there something familiar?"

"No, no. Go ahead, Lillian."

"Maybe when I get things cleaned up... I'm hoping we find some longer bones for several reasons—height, etc. Obviously, it won't happen at this 3' level, but once we go deeper, perhaps we'll find some."

Harry's face paled; if the bones were Celeste's, they weren't ready for this ending even after so many years.

Mac poured another cup of coffee. "Lillian, how long on DNA?"

"Not like television—you know that. I'll do what I can to get it as quick as possible. Something else—do you have any idea about possible cause of death? It goes without saying I will examine everything I find."

The men remained silent.

"Anyone?"

Mac looked at Harry. Not getting a response, he answered. "No, can't give you anything. We can only repeat what we talked about early on. If the victim turns out to be who we think, the young lady was fifteen when she disappeared—the cause of death could be anything from a blow on the head to buried alive."

"Since she was so young, did you consider the possibility that a foreign substance—alcohol, sedatives, etc.—could have been introduced into her bloodstream? Considering her age, I would suspect alcohol."

Harry intervened. "If this turns out to be Celeste, she wasn't a drinker—"

"No, that's not what I'm saying. I'm talking about the perpetrator doing this to her. There's a lot of ways this could happen. Just something to consider. There's been a breakthrough study on this recently. Since the suspected victim was fifteen, if a certain amount of alcohol was put into her bloodstream, it could result in death."

"Understood, but I had no idea you could go into the bone and determine this kind of thing."

Lillian grinned. "New procedures coming out all the time. Anyway, I know your time is valuable and I need to get back to work."

"You won't forget about the bug man, will you?"

"Not a chance. I need him out here when the time is right." She looked at Harry. "I don't want to cross lines here, but when something is found, I call Mac first, right?"

Harry laughed. "Right on. If you can't get the big man, call me."

Mac hurried to his car. "Harry, that was intense, wasn't it?"

"Intense doesn't begin to describe it."

FOURTEEN

He watched from the shadows of the bleachers—watched the machines digging and leveling—digging and leveling. He saw two men talking, obviously cops—he watched a woman and a man climb out of the hole with plastic bags. They wouldn't find anything important—he had been too careful—it had been too long.

FIFTEEN

Harry left Mac and Lillian with shocking mental images haunting him—too intense—he needed to dilute them. He drove through the familiar streets of the town where he was raised. He could find his way to St. Vincent's blindfolded. After all, he had gone there every Sunday since he was a kid, but today was different. He wasn't going to Mass, he just needed to see and talk to his brother. He pulled in front of the magnificent grey stone church, remembering how he used to think the steeples touched heaven. A few people coming out of the massive wood doors acknowledged him as he walked to the rectory. He rang the bell—the housekeeper, Mattie, answered.

"Harry, what a pleasant surprise. Come in out of the cold—seems old man winter is in a hurry to get here this year. Let me take your coat and have a seat in the parlor. I have a nice fire going. I'll get Father Andrew for you." She looked around at the man who looked so much like his brother. "Would you like some tea?"

"Thanks, I would. Is Father Andy busy? Sorry I didn't call ahead."

"You know he always has time for his big brother. You two don't see enough of each other. Relax, Harry. I'll get your tea and let him know you're here."

When Father Andrew walked in, Harry was on his cell. Harry turned and smiled as he slipped the phone in his pocket. "Come over here and give your brother a hug."

"Sure. Everything all right? You okay?"

"Yes, but I had a bad morning and needed a safe harbor for a while. You're it."

"Come on. You never stop by in the afternoon—are you sick?"

"No worries, little brother." Harry beat his curled fists on his chest. "Look, my body's in fine shape. It's my psyche that needs healing."

Father Andy pointed to a large overstuffed chair by the window. "Sit." He took the one next to it.

"Did I catch you at a bad time?"

"No, never a bad time for you. I was on the phone with Rachel. I'm helping her put together a fund raiser for a new hospital wing for the kids."

"Get out of here. Why didn't you tell me? I'd like to help."

"I'm counting on your help, but right now we're just in the planning stage. By the way, I've been doing some fascinating research on photos her mom took. Rachel's going to put them in an exhibition with the proceeds going to St. Clair Hospital."

"Sounds intriguing. Tell me about it."

The rattling of china drew their attention toward the door. Mattie was carrying a large silver tray holding tea and sandwiches. They both jumped to help.

"You're a dear, Mattie. How did you know I haven't had lunch?"

"I figured as much, Harry. Neither has your brother. Now both of you sit and have a nice quiet lunch together. I'll make sure no one bothers you."

"Mattie's right," Andy said. "Let's eat first and talk later."

"I'd like that."

It didn't take long for Harry to finish his sandwich and put his plate on the tray. He refilled his mug with steaming tea before sitting back. He sighed as he looked out the window at the dreary day. "Spending quiet time together—nice, Andy. We have to do it more often."

"I agree. Feel like talking now?"

"You first. Tell me about those photos."

"Come on, we'll talk about them some other time. What's troubling you?"

"I have some sad news. It looks like we may have found some of the remains of Celeste Adams."

"Dear God in heaven. That explains why you are here in the afternoon."

"Yeah, I don't know why it's so disturbing—so much time has passed—twenty-eight years. You know, we all gave up finding her alive years ago."

"I know we did, but there was always that little spark of hope that maybe, just maybe, it would turn out differently. After all, faith is what keeps us going, isn't it?"

"You're right, but what they found at the dig with her really tore me up."

"What was it?"

"I'm pretty sure it was part of the rosary dad gave her. Remember? He gave them to all our friends when you were ordained."

"What makes you think that?"

"The stones embedded in the finger bones were greenish. I'm telling you there was no mistaking the malachite beads—at least for me. Who would have thought I would find those stones in the grave of a murdered child? Hell, the rosary was supposed to protect her. Damn it, Andy, she had to be holding it when she was put in that grave. Where was He, Andy? Where was God and why didn't He help her? How many times do I have to ask these questions?"

"Every time we bury a child, Harry—that's why you're a cop and I'm a priest. That's why Michael does his radio show. It's our job. Dear Lord, she must have been terrified to be holding onto her rosary. It's small consolation, but I'd like to think the rosary gave Celeste inner peace during her dark time."

"Damn it to hell, it's getting worse instead of better. What's happening in this world?"

"Don't know, but I pray every night it will get better."

Andy got up to fill his mug. "Want more, Harry?"

"Full up. Thanks."

Andy sipped his tea. "Twenty-eight years. Every time I hear that number it hits a chord with me. I know, of course, that's how long Celeste has been missing, but it has some other significance I've not been able to figure out. Then, this morning I was working on a sermon and it hit me—Ecclesiastes."

Harry looked at Andy. "You lost me."

"Chapter three, verses two to eight. You know..." He stopped and waited for Harry to show some recognition. "Okay—a song, what's the name? Come on, brother, you know the one—'for every season turn, turn, turn or something like that.'" Andy grinned. "Don't make me sing it."

"Right, I've heard it at weddings."

"You got it. Well, I had this friend in school who was interested in numerology and we did some research. Just playing around, you know. I ended up doing a paper on symbolism in the Bible. I found some fascinating concepts."

"Like what?"

"The number seven and its compounds occur in multiples throughout the Bible—seven miracles, seven appearances of angels...on and on. Like I said, this chapter and verses in Ecclesiastes enumerates twenty-eight 'times' in these seven verses."

"Lost me again."

"'A time to be born, a time to die, a time to kill, a time to heal...' I don't know—seems strange. I've been thinking about it this morning and now this news about Celeste."

"Are we talking premonitions, little brother?"

"Maybe. I don't know. You mentioned that song is performed at weddings, but it's played even more at funerals."

Harry put on his coat. "I guess this visit just came full circle—we're talking funerals."

"Right, sorry. This all weighs heavy on my mind. I used to find peace at Mass with my congregation. Now, all I see is apprehension in their eyes—seems everyone is unsettled."

Andy walked Harry to the door with his arm around his

shoulders. "I said it earlier—things aren't getting any better. Well, would you look at us?"

"What?"

"Harry and Andy—gloom and doom." Harry punched his brother in the arm.

Andy laughed, nodding. "You're right."

"Enough already. We know it's the nature of the beast. We can't let it get us down—can't let it win. Happy thoughts, little brother."

"Right again. What's wrong with me? I'm the one who should be preaching love and happiness to you. Thanks, Harry, for the wake-up call. I'll lighten up my sermons and add some jokes."

"Heard some good ones the other day."

"Yeah, I know the kind you hear at the station." Andy grinned. "Harry, sorry but another sad note—I want to be with you when you break the news to Celeste's family."

"Wouldn't have it any other way. Just know that we are keeping everything confidential until all loose ends are tied up in a neat bundle. It won't be the happy ending we wanted, but at least it will bring closure for the family."

Sixteen

Lillian called Mac asking that he and Harry come to the site as soon as possible. She was ready for him to pry information out of her, but she stayed tight lipped.

As soon as they got out of their car, they heard her whistle. The men looked at each other and said in unison, "You gotta love her."

When they got close, Lillian held up her arms. "Hallelujah, guys. We got something."

Mac and Harry crouched at the edge of the excavation. Harry spoke first. "Lillian, is that what it looks like?"

"Yeah, a skull. It looks in decent condition. Give me a few minutes."

Lillian and her assistant, Mark, proceeded with their usual routine. Lillian then moved to the temporary ladder to get on equal ground with Mac and Harry.

"See you don't need a hand now, Lillian."

"Harry, I can always use a hand, but the ladder helps."

They looked at Mac who had knelt on one knee. "Please, dear God," he whispered.

Harry put his hand on his shoulder. "Easy, man. Don't jump to conclusions."

"I know it's Celeste's—don't ask me how I know. I just know. I've got a terrible emptiness in the pit of my stomach." He stood taking a deep breath as he brushed his pants off. "Okay, sorry. What's next, Lillian?"

"Let's go to the lab and talk." Once inside Lillian said, "Mark should have the skull in here soon. In the meantime, to answer your question, Mac—my next step is to reconstruct the skull. You know how that works, so no need to bore you with the details. You're lucky, though…"

"We know that."

"What I was going to say, gentlemen, I've had extensive training in facial reconstruction—this can tell us a lot about the victim. "We also found a partial hair on one piece of the skull. Mark will bring that in too. I can tell you that it looks dark brown." She pulled out the examination table as she talked.

Harry spoke with a touch of relief and sadness in his voice. "If it's brown, it can't be Celeste Adams'. Her hair was golden."

Lillian stared intently at Harry. "You know as well as I do that if that particular hair has been in the ground for a long time, we can't tell about the color until we do some tests. Don't get encouraged or discouraged until we know more. Anything is possible under these circumstances."

Mark came in with the specimens. He went about his business of laying the skull and hair on the table for Lillian's examination and tests. She was silent for a few minutes. "I'm jumping the gun here, men, but before you ask me…"

Mac chuckled. "You're getting to know me, aren't you?"

"A little bit. The DNA…"

"We talked about that earlier."

"Yes, we did. I wanted to remind you, though, we should be able to extract DNA from a tooth formation and from the skull itself. We'll see."

Several days passed before Mac got a call from Bill who confirmed he and his crew had created a depth of 6' across the grid area.

"I'm calling for Lillian, Mac. Hold onto your badge—we've got news."

"Let's hear it."

"We found another skull."

"A-another—what the hell?" Mac tripped over his words.

"Lillian has her hands full, but she wants you guys out here ASAP."

Mac and Harry were at Concord in thirty minutes. Mac brought Harry up-to-date on the way.

"Man, is it possible another person was buried in this unholy of graves? My chest aches at what this could mean—another lost soul?"

"Mac, I can't friggin' believe it."

"After I talked to Bill, I started wondering if maybe—just maybe—they've unearthed an old unmarked cemetery. Possible?"

"Holy hell, wouldn't that be something? If that's the case, it could be another dead end for the Adams family."

Mac pointed to the end of the grid area. "There's Lillian, in the dirt as usual."

Before they could get to her section, Bill approached them. "Mac, this is damn unnerving—to find two skulls and in a relatively short time."

"It's damn unbelievable. I want to run something by you, Bill. I imagine you have unearthed old cemeteries in your time."

"Not many but a few. We've encountered this on commercial construction a time or two where we've gone way down in the ground. You're thinking this is what's happening here?"

"Just wondering—that's all."

"We haven't found any pieces of granite or other material used in tombstones. Even if the markers were wooden, we would find some scratching on them to indicate names. Of course, varmints make short work of wooden markers—carry them off and so on. I remember hearing about a case where they discovered the remains of a Civil War era cemetery."

"Sure 'nuff, Bill?"

"Yeah, but there were only a few markers they could make out. I should add that this discovery was made by a large exploration company doing commercial excavations and that runs deep as I said. It wasn't anything like we're doing at Concord."

"Thanks. Finding the second skull got me thinking."

Once Lillian climbed out of the sunken area, she took one look at Mac and Harry and held up her hand. "Don't even say it. I know you want something on this one like, yesterday."

"Sorry to push." Mac raised his arms toward the sky and then let them fall to his sides. "Lillian, could this area be an old grave site?"

"Too soon to tell."

Harry nodded.

Lillian studied their somber faces. "Guys, I don't care how many times you see this stuff, it never gets easier."

"You got that right," Harry said. "It's the end of the day. We're officially off duty—let's grab a drink. Join us, Lil?"

"Are you kidding? I've got work to do."

When Mac got to the precinct the next morning, he left orders at the front desk not to be disturbed for thirty minutes. In the meantime, Lillian called and left word.

"Lil, sorry you had to wait. Something going on?"

"Are you and Harry coming out today?"

"Silly question. We're coming out, but not sure when. Harry's meeting with the Chief about the case he was working on when I roped him into this one. I could come now, but I'd just have to repeat everything to Harry later."

"Not necessary. Come together when you can."

Mac cleared his desk in the afternoon, grabbed Harry, and headed to the construction site. As soon as the men stepped into the mobile unit, Lillian eagerly engaged them in her work.

"The first thing I want to tell you is that both victims suffered trauma to the head. The first skull we found was in fair condition, which made it easier to see. The second one was in pieces, but when I laid it out, I could tell a blunt instrument had been used on the cranium."

"In other words," Mac said, "something creased the victims' skulls?"

"Yes, something heavy. I've made impressions of the young

victims' dental work and teeth formations. If we can't get enough DNA from the skull and other material, we can canvas dentists and odontologists in the area. Anyway, it's all in my report. If you want, I can give you the details now. Do you want them now?"

"No, not now. Your report will be fine unless you need an okay to proceed with something." Mac faced Lil. "You said young person. Explain the *young* part."

"I base this on bone development. It's difficult to be absolutely accurate because people mature at different rates. I've seen some kids whose anatomy was fully developed at age fifteen or sixteen. On the other hand, I've seen some who didn't mature until they were closer to twenty or so. It varies.

"Can you give me anything else on identities?"

"Not much more than what we've already discussed. We reopened a possible homicide case that took place in 1979 and we're hoping, not actually hoping—guess you know what I mean… Anyway, a young woman, fifteen year old Celeste Adams, disappeared around that time. We have reason to believe she was the victim of a homicide."

"Thanks for that much."

Nothing had been the same for Mac or Harry since the department reopened Celeste Adams' case. Mac lived every day with expectations and hopes mixed with dread and he knew Harry did too. Every time Lillian Katz called, his stomach turned waiting for the unpredictable.

Her call today was no different. Lillian asked them to come to the site as soon as they could clear their desks. Once they were in the lab, Lillian said, "Mac, Harry, the first skull we found is that of Celeste Adams."

"You sure?"

"Positive ID. We confirmed identification from dental work after you gave me the girl's name."

Mac sunk into a nearby chair and put his head in his hands. "Dear God, I knew it!" He looked at Lillian. "It makes me sick."

He scrutinized Harry's face, a reflection of his own. "Okay, what about the second? Any matches?"

"Not yet. My next step is reconstruction. Do you want to run a check on dentist's offices now?"

"Hold off on that. Do the reconstruction first." He moved toward the coffee bar. "Mind if I grab a cup of the black stuff?"

"Help yourself, but I have a better suggestion. Why don't we take a break and go up the street to that small coffee shop—can't think of the name."

"Good idea. Harry, have time?"

"Yeah, if we make it short."

Mac signaled with a raised thumb. "Hold on a minute, you two. Lillian, I mentioned that I went to school with Celeste Adams, didn't I?" He waited for acknowledgement before continuing. "This case would be hard even if I didn't know the victim, but since I knew her, it's double hard."

Lillian rubbed his shoulder. "I'm sorry. You know our work has to stay impersonal, but there are times it can't. Look at the positive side. You are finally finding out what happened to the young girl all those years ago."

"I know all the platitudes, but I *knew* her, Lillian. Harry too. He's been close to Celeste's family for years. Long story short, I fantasized about a future with her. She was kind to me. I didn't have many friends in high school. The kids made fun of my clothes and called me 'four eyes' because of my thick glasses. Celeste made time to talk to me and ate lunch with me most days. Our lockers were close together and she'd stand there talking after school until her boyfriend, Ted Burton, came along."

Harry punched Mac in the ribs. "Looking at this handsome fellow now, you'd never think he was called four eyes, would you, Lil?"

She smiled and took Mac's arm. "Absolutely not. Come on, men, let's get that coffee. I'd like to hear more about this young woman whose life ended much too soon."

SEVENTEEN

Harry replayed Lillian's words over and over in his head, "...the first skull we found is that of Celeste Adams." He knew it would be from the time he saw the green stones in the finger bones. It was time he came clean with Mac and Lillian. His visit with Andy gave him the boost he needed.

He should have taken care of this the first moment he saw the stones, but he couldn't get the words out, and he knew why. If he admitted he recognized the stones, it meant the bones belonged to Celeste. He needed time to digest the finality of the situation. Now, with the positive ID of the first skull, he still had to take care of telling Mac and Lillian about the rosary.

He went by Mac's office and found him poring through Celeste's file. If Mac wasn't at Concord, he had his nose in this file or staring at the cards on his cork board. *I'm just as bad. I can't get any of this out of my mind either. Joan helped, Andy helped, but the vision of those bones are as embedded in my mind as the stones are in the bones.*

Mac looked up and motioned toward one of his chairs. "What's up, man?"

Harry shook his head and strolled toward the window.

"Sit. You look like you could use a break," Mac said.

"I'd rather stand. I have something to tell you and I should have done it a few days ago."

"Sounds serious."

"Something I've put off talking about, that's all." Harry looked out the window again before starting. "It's about the stones embedded in the finger bones."

"Yeah, I know about the stones."

"What you don't know is that I recognized them."

"What the hell?"

"What the hell is right, Mac. Let me tell you a story. When my brother, Andy, was ordained all my family went to his ordination in Rome."

"Yeah, know about that too. What does his ordination have to do with the bones?"

"A lot. My dad gave rosaries to those who made the trip, Michael—"

"Celeste? My God."

"Yes, Celeste. My mother wanted green stones for the rosary beads. She wanted green to represent Ireland. She chose malachite."

"Anything else different about the rosaries?"

"I don't know if you are familiar with a rosary..."

"I am. They seem to be part of the uniform with some of my men."

"Okay, the only difference with these—they were one decade instead of the usual five. The center image differed for the boys and girls. For the girls, mother put an image of Our Lady of Fatima with Andy's ordination date on the reverse side."

"Lillian hasn't found that medal."

"Not that we know of, at least yet."

"You don't have to say anything more. Celeste had the rosary in her hands..."

"I'm sure of it. You remember what Lil said about extreme pressure. She had to be praying when that dirt was piled on her."

"Stop it! I've got the picture."

"Only consolation—she was praying."

"Okay, what about the cross? Was it on the table?"

"No, I would have picked up on it. I need to tell Lillian about this—she's still finding miscellaneous items. I think her assistant,

Mark, found some more stuff the other day. I need to get out there and fill her in. Want to come along?"

"Try and keep me away."

When Mac and Harry arrived at the site, they checked the excavation area first. Lillian's assistant told them she was in the lab.

After the usual hellos, Lillian pointed at the recently found objects. "I need you two to check those out. See if there's anything you recognize."

Harry moved closer to Lillian. "Lil, there's something we, guess I should say I, need to tell you."

"Don't know if I like the sound of that. What's going on?"

"It's about the stones in the finger bones."

"Yeah and you're going to tell me they're malachite."

"You already know?"

"I do. After I cleaned the bones and, of course, extracted the stones, I ran some tests. They are malachite. Now, what about them?"

Harry repeated the ordination story to Lillian. "Have you found any round medals like one would find on a rosary—or a cross?"

"Check out the work area to the left of the skeletal remains. Mark brought in some more items earlier. They need to be cleaned, but it won't take long to do it." Lillian sat in the chair and after awhile put both thumbs in the air. "Again, you two must be living right."

"Why's that?"

"Because we may have found one of the items you asked about, Harry."

Harry clasped his hands behind his back and moved around the table. "Won't touch. Promise. You know, Lil, you remind me of my mother when I was a little boy. Every time she took my brother and me shopping, she went through the same routine. 'Don't touch anything, boys. If you break something, I'll have to buy it.' Believe me, I get the message."

Lillian laughed softly. "Now you're calling me a mother?"

Mac interrupted. "Hold it, you two. There's the cross, Harry. Lillian, hand me that magnifying glass, would you?"

Harry grabbed it out of his hand. "Me first. I see it. Man, it looks in pretty good shape."

"You can say that again. I'd say it's in better than good shape." Lillian grabbed another magnifying glass. "You can see every detail—even the tiny nails in Jesus' hands. Unbelievable. Okay, check for the medal you described."

"Nope, don't see it." He looked at Lillian with a sideways grin. He saw her smile. "What is it, Lil?"

"Old times, that's all."

Mac chimed in. "Back to the medal. Can't have everything. It may show up later, but it would be very small, huh, Harry?"

"Hmmm?"

"It would be small, right?"

"I heard you, Mac. Yes. I know the links connecting the beads to the medal and cross can be disengaged easily. I don't know what kind of varmints are down in the ground, but I'm sure there are some…"

"Harry, anything can happen underground. Don't forget they were putting in the tennis courts twenty-eight years ago, a lot of digging and redistribution of dirt. It's hard to tell."

Harry took a long look at the cross. "I had to see it for my-self—didn't want to believe it. There is no question that's the ro-sary my dad gave Celeste."

"You know we've already identified Celeste."

"I know it, dammit, but it's hard to put into my head. The rosary…"

"Harry, why don't you sit?"

"God, I wish you two could convince me the ID is wrong and it's not Celeste's rosary. Tell me it's *all* wrong for godsakes."

"We can't."

Mac and Lillian stared in silence.

EIGHTEEN

Those dimwits. I can walk around this school or anywhere else when I damn well feel like it. No one notices me. They think they're so superior. Truth is, I'm too smart for all of them.

NINETEEN

Mac reviewed the recent Hornsby/Milford High case, scribbling a note on the side of the yellow pad: *lot of similarities to Celeste, check board.* It didn't surprise him young Pam Hornsby had been seen in the company of some of Concord's cheerleaders and Concord's coach, Ted Burton, after several football games.

Mac pushed his pencil through the paper. "I can't friggin' believe Burton's name pops up everywhere these days." Mac buzzed John and Ed. "Guys, you're doing a phenomenal job on the Hornsby case. What's on your plate for the rest of the day?"

The officers grinned at each other and then at Mac. John fell against the wall grabbing his chest. "Ed, did he say phenomenal?"

"I think that's what he said."

"Well, Mac, we can't f'n believe it. Would you say it again?"

Mac opened the file. "Come on, you act like I never compliment you. Let's put our heads together. Anything new other than what's in the file?"

The men sank in chairs across from Mac. "Wish we could say we had more, but what you see is what we have—slim pickings. Guess you noticed Hornsby was seen in Burton's company a couple of times."

"Yep. As coach of Concord's football team, that bastard's always going to be around cheerleaders—even those from other schools. Normally, I wouldn't be concerned about the coach/cheerleader association, but with Burton in the mix?"

Ed grinned. "Talking about cheerleaders, Burton has been seen around with Sarah Gibbons."

"Should I know her?"

"Yeah, she's in the file—she was Pam Hornsby's cheerleading coach."

"Okay, boss-man, when are you going to talk to Burton? You think he's also involved in the Hornsby/Milford High case?"

"Could be, but we have to play it safe. He's well respected in the community. He's secure in his job—he's not going anywhere. Remember, he likes being Number 1."

"So, when are you going to talk to him?"

"Let's dig some more. I'll let you know in a few days."

The next morning brought another wave of cold air, cold enough for Jack Frost to do some serious work and paint everything in sight. Harry strode into Mac's office and watched him for a few minutes before speaking. "Hey, man, this cold blast worrying you? It's not all that bad."

Mac turned and his expression said it all. "I know. I was just looking at the frosted window, beautiful but a prelude to death—death of the few remaining fall leaves and flowers."

"Aren't you poetic this morning?"

"Well, we have a man out there who is as hard and cold as that frozen water and I'd like to be the one who puts him on ice permanently."

"Man, oh man, you're in a mood, but I don't blame you. We're walking around in a nightmare here." Harry leaned on one of the chairs. "There's something I want to talk to you about."

"Go ahead."

"Not until you pull yourself away from that chilling scene." He watched Mac slide into his chair before beginning.

"When are you going to talk to Burton?"

"Actually, I plan on delegating that task to John and Ed."

"You seriously think Burton could be responsible for the Hornsby girl's disappearance?"

"I do, but can't connect the dots yet."

"The only dot I can see, Mac, is the cheerleading dot."

"You think it's time? We don't want to scare him away."

"You won't—he's too much of a pompous ass."

After Mac delegated the Burton interview to John and Ed, he received word from them sooner than expected. He and Harry were finishing their survey of Concord's site when the men's call came through. He gave a thumbs up to Harry as he agreed to meet the guys at a diner around the corner.

Once the four men were settled in a booth at the small cafe, John and Ed tossed a coin to see who would begin.

Mac winked at Harry. "Funny, guys. You two practicing a comedy act? Let us have it. Was Burton surprised to see you?"

"Not at all. The guy acted like he expected someone from the police long before this. The same went for the other teachers we talked to. The only one who seemed unsettled was the principal, Mr. McCoy."

"What do you make of that?"

"Not anything right now. He got a little angry we were, as he put it, 'poking around the school'."

"I've talked to McCoy before—he's kinda an odd duck. Anyway, back to Burton."

"He acted cool like there was nothing we could say that would shake him up."

"That's our boy."

Ed rubbed his hands together. "If it's him, Mac, we'll get him, but I'm not so sure."

"Why?"

"Because, I hate to keep saying this, he's more the lover boy type. He looks like he wouldn't want to dirty his hands, if you know what I mean."

Mac sipped his coffee. "Wow, hot! I still think he's our man. There's no doubt he's a womanizer, but that doesn't change anything. Did he comment about talking to Bill at the site?"

"Nope, he didn't say a word. Take it back—he did say that he had gone over there with some of the teachers about a week ago. He asked what was going on and you know our answer."

"Any signs of nervousness?"

"None."

"I almost forgot, Ed. Was there anyone on Concord's staff who had worked there in '79?"

"There was an older lady, Rosa Ingram. She's been the librarian since '70."

"So?"

"So, she remembered Celeste Adams because the young girl loved books and liked discussing the classics with her. We asked if she ever saw Celeste with any boys. She was nervous about mentioning Burton because he's on staff now and he has a lot of pull as we all know. Nevertheless, she told us she's pretty sure she caught the two of them huddled together more than once, but she reminded us of her age. Of course, she made us promise not to say anything about this."

"And like good policemen, you promised?"

"Yeah, we promised."

"Okay, she put Celeste and Burton together—we already knew that. Back to the Hornsby case, what was Burton's reaction to her name?"

Ed spoke up, "He stammered around, insisting he didn't know her."

"Did you find Sarah Gibbons?"

"We called her at Milford High and she agreed to meet with us."

"And?"

"You'd be proud of us, Mac. We did a damn good job of playing good cop/bad cop."

Harry raised his eyebrow. "How did that work?"

"Yeah, fill us in." Mac added.

Ed chuckled. "The first things we noticed were her big blue eyes and long blonde hair."

Mac looked disgusted. "Seriously, guys…"

"No, Mac. It hit us—they…"

"Hold on, what do you mean, they?"

"Miss Gibbons had photographs of cheerleaders hanging all around her office and they all looked like they fell out of the same mold. That included Gibbons."

"Explain."

"The girls all looked related."

Harry watched them go back and forth. "Long blonde hair, big blue eyes—well, that fits Pam and Celeste. Maybe you guys are onto something."

"That's what we thought."

"Okay, men, give it up on Sarah Gibbons."

"Ed started out belittling Burton and she came to his defense. I, of course, praised him saying he was the Number One coach in the district and so on. That's all it took for her to get on my side."

Mac reacted. "She liked him?"

"Hell, yeah, it was written all over her face, but she was very guarded."

"Good job, guys."

TWENTY

Mac looked up from his paperwork to see Michael Adams and his father coming through the door.

"Hey, Mac, we thought you were going to keep us posted. Any progress?"

"Have a seat, gentlemen. It's good to see you up and around, Mike. How are you feeling?"

"Better. They can't keep me down forever, you know. I'm not back where I want to be yet, but I'm getting there." Michael shot a sideways glance at his dad. "What do you think, am I back to normal?"

Jim patted his son's shoulder, letting his hand linger longer than usual. "Son, some might say you were never normal, but your mother and I love you just the same."

"I was going to call you both later this morning." He paused watching their expressions change.

"What do you have?"

"I wanted to tell you we're making progress..."

"What does 'making progress' mean?"

Mac leaned back in his chair and smiled. "This reminds me of our first conversation about your sister. You just won't let me finish a story."

Michael smiled. "*Mea culpa.* You have the floor."

"That's all I have to say—we're making progress and we want to bring this case to a close before long. Look, men, you've waited

28 years and I'll be damned if I come to you with anything but complete closure."

Jim stood up and extended his hand. "Mac, you and Harry are doing a damn good job."

"Thanks, Jim. I can assure you we're trying our best. Now, Michael, when are you going back to work?"

"Actually, I'm going back tomorrow to thank everyone for their support and let them know I'm going to take a sabbatical. I need to spend time with my family and be with Chris during his rehab."

Jim fixed his eyes on Mike. "Besides that, son, you need time for your own rehab."

Mac forced a smile. "Mike, Jim—you and your family have been through a lot. You all need time off. Trust me here."

TWENTY-ONE

Michael walked into the radio station early afternoon among cheers of welcome and smiling faces. He forced tears away to make this a happy occasion, but it was heavy stuff and he didn't feel up to the task. Sadness surrounding the shooting scene still defied explanation. He was relieved the staff understood how difficult it would be for him to handle his first broadcast.

He spotted Bob by the snack table with the widest grin he had ever seen on his face. He motioned him to meet him half-way. After a bear hug, he whispered in his ear, "Why didn't you tell me about this?"

Bob guided him to the front of the room. "Folks, after all these years, I think we finally overwhelmed Mike. We'll keep this brief and try to avoid all the mushy-gushy stuff—or maybe we won't." He looked at Michael. "Buddy, we can't avoid sentimental-ity when it comes to what you've been through. Our hearts have been heavy since we first received news of Concord's shooting and while you and your son fought for your lives. We all mourned the loss of the young people that died that day. Today though is a day of thanksgiving and celebration for you and your family.

"Mike, we all love you, we love Rachel, we love Chris and your other children." He hesitated. "Sorry, folks, but Mike's not the only one overwhelmed." He looked around the room. "I can see we all are." He picked up a glass of iced tea. "Sorry we can't have anything stronger, but work you know? Anyway, lift a glass and celebrate Michael Adams' return to the fold." Bob waited a few seconds. "Michael, my dear friend and colleague, we toast you and your family and wish good health and happiness in the future."

When Michael looked at his co-workers in front of him, he was visibly shaken. "I don't know if I can top that speech, Bob, but I'll try. My family and I appreciate all your prayers, more than I can say today. We have gone through difficult times, but, thank God, Chris is recovering and you can't keep me down for long—guess you all know that.

"Seriously, I couldn't ask for a better group of people than all of you. It's not only during this tragic time that you've stepped up, but you give a hundred percent every day we work together. We only grow stronger and stronger. I'm happy to be part of this station's family and I want to continue to share each other's ideas and strengths for many years to come."

He glanced at Bob, walked to his side and put his arm around his shoulders. "I know everyone is aware of this man's technical and creative ability, but I would like to add to those qualities by telling you he has been part of my family throughout this disaster—sitting by my bed, cracking jokes, cheering up my wife as much as possible, getting me water when my throat was dry, feeding me…believe me, that was the final straw." Mike patted Bob's shoulder. "I don't want to embarrass you, or maybe I do. Anyway, thanks buddy, for staying by my side throughout this ordeal and keeping all these folks informed.

"My sincere appreciation to each and every one of you. Now, I need to prepare for tonight. So, back to work."

Bob turned to Mike. "I'm part of your family?"

"Yeah, but don't let it go to your head."

"Mike, I'm usually not an overemotional kind of guy, but…"

"You don't have to say anything. I meant every word I said about you. Rachel and I depended on you more than you know during this battle to regain our senses and you did as much for me as any brother would do."

Bob touched his hand to his heart. "I can't talk about this any more. Get on with your preparation."

Michael opened his evening broadcast with intense fervor. "Good evening to all. I prepared some opening remarks earlier, but now...now I'd rather just talk. To say I've missed you is an understatement. This period in the lives of my family has been excruciating and painful beyond belief, but thanks to our family, good friends, co-workers at the station, and best wishes from my listeners, we have finally walked into a light that is bright and full of promise.

"This broadcast is different from those in the past, as I said before, and I hope you will indulge me in sharing some personal thoughts with you. You don't hear much about the staff who make this program happen, but they are always here, always making sure we put on the best informative radio show we can. I promise you we take our commitment to you, our listening audience, very seriously and EPOH will continue that commitment.

"Now, for a few personal statements. I usually keep my religious convictions to myself because I believe this is an individual's prerogative, but I am a man of strong faith. Without this faith, I promise you that Rachel, Chris, and I could not have survived our recent ordeal. The station kept me apprised of your phone calls and emails. I want to say thank you one and all.

"Our director, Bob Matthews, keeps me, as well as everyone at the station on track. He wants to address you on this special night, so now I turn the program over to him."

Bob cleared his throat. "Ladies and gentlemen, we at EPOH want to add our sincere appreciation to all of you for being part of our listening audience. Michael Adams' broadcast is one presented from the heart while staying within the boundaries of a radio newscast. He and his family have experienced a terrible ordeal during the recent past and all our station's employees have missed him more than I can say. I know from your emails and letters that you have too.

"At this time, Michael will take a sabbatical from the station to take care of his family. We are pleased to tell you we have several visiting hosts who will continue with enlightening programs. We know you will miss Michael Adams, but rest assured he will be back with us before long with a fresh agenda. So, stay tuned and keep Michael's family in your thoughts and prayers. Now Michael has some closing statements."

"Thank you Bob. There is another issue I feel I must address tonight. We have had hundreds of inquires about our mystery caller Celeste. Many believe she made an appearance at the school shooting as the medic that helped save my son Chris. Also, there here have been reports that this woman we know as Celeste was involved in a miracle. As far as we know, this is all speculation. No one has come up with a definitive explanation and no one has seen or heard from this woman. Sorry to report, we have no answers. So, I will close the show tonight with a question for you. Do you believe in miracles? Take care and keep the faith. Goodnight."

He looked at the control booth—Bob lifted his arm and rotated his wrist. "Mike, we're off air, but you have one more call."

"Michael Adams here. May I help you?"

"Oh, yes, you can if only you would," a velvet tone voice responded.

"Alex? That you?"

"How could you mistake my voice? Of course it's me. How are you, Michael?"

His voice chilled. "Quite well. More importantly, how are *you* since you stomped out of the station in a childish rage?"

"Things work out for the best. Guess the station has decided not to sue—I haven't received anything, at least not yet."

"If you're calling to get this information, I can't help you."

"I knew Bob wouldn't put me through during air time," she purred, "but that's okay. I wanted to tell you I was snatched up by a Houston television station. They recognize my worth, Michael, more than I can say for your affiliation."

"Good to hear all is going well for you. I appreciate your call. Good—"

"Hold on, big boy. I want to know how things are going for you and your charming wife."

"There's nothing more to say except to wish you luck. I'm hanging up now, Alex."

Michael looked up toward Bob, but he didn't have to look far. Bob was at his elbow making all kinds of faces. "Why didn't you get her number?"

"Man, you don't know when you're well off. Forget that woman and get on with your life."

"That's the trouble—I don't have a life to get on with."

"Don't forget the nice looking nurse."

"You said it all there—nice looking. I need more than that and Alex is the whole package."

"What about her ducking out on her contract?"

"The big boys decided to let it go—not worth the expense. She's a closed book as far as business is concerned, but I'd still like to get something going. Who knows? Now that she's away from here, maybe."

"Man, if anyone was ever bewitched by a woman, you're it."

TWENTY-TWO

Mac popped into Concord toward the end of the day on Tuesday. He knew Burton's schedule took him to the gym about four o'clock. He wouldn't expect him—maybe something could come of the surprise.

When he opened the gym door, Burton was in a huddle with some of the players. As soon as Burton saw him, he grinned broadly and headed his way. "Hey, Officer Mac, long time no see. Are you looking for anyone in particular?"

"You bet I am, Ted. It's you."

Mac watched Burton saunter away from the players. He looked every bit the cool man he remembered from high school days. He knew Burton remembered him from Concord too—he was always telling him to stay away from Celeste. *I want to slither into his insides and set him off. If he knows why I'm here, he's hiding it well.*

"What can I do for you, Officer?"

"Is there somewhere we can go for privacy?"

"Sorry, as you can see I'm working…coaching one of the best teams in the State. I love working with these kids."

Mac got into his face. "Don't push me, I need a few minutes of your time—make it happen."

Burton swallowed hard, hissing under his breath, "Bastard." He called over his assistant and ordered him to take the team out and start doing laps. Burton led the way to a back office.

"Okay, *now* what can I do for you?"

Mac refused to be rushed. He wanted to make him squirm. He continued to stare at Burton.

"Officer?"

"Yes?"

Burton flashed the smile that garnered all the young girls in the old days and laughed slightly. "Sorry, your last name?"

"It's Hudson."

"Well, Officer Mac Hudson, what can I do for you?"

"I imagine you could do a lot of things for me, Teddy, but the question is—will you?"

Burton's face reddened. "I'd prefer you not call me Teddy, if you don't mind. It takes me back to a not too happy childhood if you know what I mean?"

"Actually, I don't. Why don't you tell me about yourself."

"Look, I don't know what this is about, but you came into the gym unannounced and requested a private area. Now, what the hell do you want?"

"What I want is very simple. I want you to tell me about your relationship with Celeste Adams."

"Celeste Adams? My God, I haven't thought about Celeste in years."

"Really? Well, you do remember the young lady, don't you?"

"Of course, I do." Burton poured a glass of water. "Help yourself if you want any. Look, let's stop this game. I remember you, Mac Hudson, from high school days."

"You do? I'm surprised."

"The reason I remember you is because you were always hanging around Celeste. Every time I saw her in the cafeteria or in the halls—there you were. She hated you, you know."

Mac struggled to keep his temper under wraps. "No, I think you're wrong about that, Teddy."

"I have to get back to my job. What do you want?"

"I would like you to tell me about what you were doing the last few months before Celeste disappeared."

"You're one crazy bastard. You tell me what you were doing back then. The cops should be investigating you, the psycho that never gets the girl."

Mac clenched his teeth, he took a few steps toward him. "I'm the one asking questions here, Mr. Burton. Concentrate— you were a senior, you were dating Celeste Adams, you broke up with her and went your merry way. Tell me about the break-up or can't you remember?"

Burton backed down realizing he had pushed Mac to his limit. "I'm glad to cooperate with the police any way I can, but I don't honestly understand what I can tell you that you don't already know."

"Give it a try."

"Celeste and I had some good times, but she was too young, too immature for me. I was getting ready to graduate, concentrating on my college scholarship, and my future. All she was interested in was being with me every minute of every day. Guess you know how that is." Burton hesitated, "Or maybe not. She wanted to get married. Can you believe that? She was just a sophomore in high school, I was graduating and moving on and she wanted to get married."

"What happened after you turned her down? I guess you *did* turn her down, didn't you?"

"Of course. What happened next was I went on with my life and she left town."

"Tell me about her leaving town."

"Nothing to tell. One day she was here, one day she wasn't. She talked a lot about living in Colorado and I imagine that's where she went. If her folks don't know, how would I?"

"Because she loved you."

"Love? Man, we're talking high school here. What the hell did any of us know about love? I'm getting sick and tired of your... what would you call them—insinuations?"

"Ted, that young girl would have done anything you wanted her to do."

Burton grinned like they were two guys in a locker room talking about their escapades. "Yeah, you got that right."

"Did you share sexual intimacy?"

Burton laughed. "Share sexual intimacy? Man, don't hold it against me, but you're just as nerdy as you were in high school. If you're asking me if we slept together, I don't think I want to answer that or any more questions without an attorney. Why are you gunning for me?"

"I'm not doing anything of the sort." Mac took his cell phone out and studied it while he savored upsetting Burton's day. "That's it for now, but we'll be back in touch." Mac shoved his card in front of Burton. "Let me know if you remember anything else about Miss Adams."

Mac left satisfied he had given Ted something to think about. He wouldn't doubt he'd even contact a lawyer.

TWENTY-THREE

Harry didn't wait to take a chair before starting with Mac. "What's up?"

Mac grinned. "Here goes. There was a notation in the original file that one of the cops…"

"Gil?"

"No, I think his name was Thompson. Anyway, he said that after Celeste disappeared, this guy, Fritz, came to the station worried about his daughter. He acted concerned that if someone hurt Celeste, they could come after his daughter next since she was Celeste's friend."

Harry shuffled in the chair. "Mac, we went over this before."

"I know, but it's time to locate his daughter, Tracy. I called him this morning—he's willing to talk to us. Tell me more about him. Do you think he stayed in touch with her?" He handed Harry the file. "Read some of the notes—jog your brain. Then, I need you to go out there with me—I don't want to spook the old guy."

Harry put on his glasses and read from the files…*he blamed himself for needing help around the place…didn't have money to hire anyone. So, that help had to come from his daughter. His wife left him about the time his daughter was starting high school.*

A second notation—the same as the first. *He acted like he blamed himself for needing help around the place, but he didn't have money to hire anyone. So, again that help had to come from his daughter, Tracy.*

He looked at Mac. "Gil was tough on him, I felt sorry for the guy. He said he wasn't used to talking to cops. That's understandable. He kept saying he was worried about his daughter. The guy heaped a lot of guilt on his shoulders for making Tracy help out so much on the farm. Anyway, he said Celeste's parents allowed her to come out to the farm once in a while and spend the night. Apparently she loved helping Tracy with chores—something different for a girl like Celeste—then they'd hit the books.

"Fritz said he kept close tabs on his daughter and that's why he eavesdropped on the girls' conversation one evening." Harry scanned the notes. "Here it is... *He was in the kitchen when he heard them giggling. He said he was embarrassed about listening but did it anyway. The Adams girl kept mentioning a boy named Ted. She called him Teddy and she kept gushing over Teddy this and Teddy that, like he was the only boy at Concord. He said Celeste convinced his daughter to try out for the cheerleading squad. He was torn when she made it, but he grudgingly gave her time off from her chores.*

"Mac, something else that's not in the file. Fritz said he heard enough to know that Celeste had been playing around with Teddy. He knew her parents wouldn't let her out of the house if they knew. He wanted to do something about it, but didn't because he didn't want his daughter to know he had been eavesdropping. Besides that, he didn't think it was any of his business."

"Lame excuse."

Mac looked steadily into Harry's eyes. "If he had taken action with Celeste's parents, maybe the girl would still be with us."

"You can't know that. After all, as far as Fritz was concerned at the time, Celeste and Tracy were just two high school girls talking about cheerleading and guys. Why would he think something bad would happen?"

"Right. Girls giggle and talk about boyfriends all the time. Ask any father of teenagers." Mac hesitated. "Did you talk to Tracy that day?"

"No, he said he sent her to her aunt's...again, concerned for her safety."

"Not to her mom's house?"

Harry laid the files down on Mac's desk. "No, it says her aunt's. I guess Gil never followed up. Remember Fritz's wife left him—probably ran as far as she could from him and that farm, just like his daughter."

Mac grabbed his coffee mug. "Let's get a caffeine fix, then head out. Maybe we'll catch the old man in a good mood."

It wasn't long before Mac and Harry settled in the car. Mac spoke first. "How about giving me Fritz' address? I'll put it in my GPS. I get all turned around on those country roads."

"Sure. I know it's out on Rt. 77 somewhere. Hold on. I'll get Fritz's file out of my briefcase."

They drove in silence most of the way.

"Mac, guess you knew Tracy."

"Yeah, I knew her because she was Celeste's friend."

"Well, then, you must have gone out to Fritz's farm back then."

Mac's voice was edgy. "I could have—don't remember."

"What the hell. This isn't an interrogation. I'm just trying to get some information on the family, damn it."

"Harry, save your questions for the old man."

"What's wrong with you?"

"I'm not looking forward to this meeting—too many memories."

"Memories of what? Celeste, Tracy, the farm?"

"I told you. Save your questions for Fritz. I'm tired of you putting me on the hot seat."

Harry faced Mac, gripping the dashboard. "I ask a few questions and I'm putting you on the hot seat? Man, that's all in your head. You better pull it together before we get there." Harry settled back in his seat, wondering what *was* in Mac's head. He had put up a shield.

Another 15 minutes went by before Mac announced, "Looks like we're here." He pulled off the road next to an old battered mailbox sadly proclaiming the home of the Fritz's. He turned sharply onto the dirt driveway. "Let's get this over with."

Choking dust bellowed around the car as they passed a decaying fence. Once they rounded the second bend, the house and barn came into view.

Mac parked the car and sat absorbing the scene. Hidden behind tall grass and weeds stood a weather-beaten, tattered shell of what was once a stately farmhouse. A few shutters hung on for dear life by a rusty nail or two. Its grimy, ashen shade made it hard to tell if the house or barn had ever seen a coat of paint. An obsolete tractor, oxidized from many spring rains and winter snows, crumbled in the field.

"This how you remember it?"

"The old man used to keep the grass cut and it had a few more shutters I think, but, yeah, same old gloomy place."

"Look, Harry, sorry for the way I've been acting. I usually keep a professional distance in cases I work, but this one is different."

"Forget it, Mac. You're a good cop. Sometimes we have to push harder, and set our emotions aside, to get the job done." Harry gave him the once-over. "Listen, man, if it starts getting to you, walk out and let me handle it. Okay? Now, ready to go in?"

"Let's do it."

A screen door slammed. The old man stood on the porch, leaning against a broken pillar.

Harry took the lead. "Hello, Mr. Fritz."

As they walked up to him, Mac noticed how disheveled he looked. He had on a T-shirt under his coveralls yellowed from grime, sweat, and absence of soap. When he got closer, Harry collided into a strong, rancid odor that floated around him. Everything about him had a sick gray pallor, from his grizzled hair to his complexion.

Mac motioned to Harry to lead the way.

"Glad you have time to talk to us, sir. I'd like you to meet Detective Mac Hudson."

Fritz shook hands and motioned them to come inside. As they walked in, they were greeted by the same sour smell that clung to the farmer. It permeated the house. It took a few seconds for

Mac's eyes to adjust to the dimly lit room. He glanced at Harry to see if he was having the same trouble.

"Have a seat," Fritz motioned to the chairs. Mac sat, Harry remained standing.

Mac opened his brief case and started going over a section of files with Fritz while Harry wandered around the small, shabby living room.

Fritz answered Mac's questions, but kept a nervous eye on Harry.

A bookcase at the far corner of the room housed what looked like family pictures. As Harry walked toward it, Fritz stood up. "How about I get you boys something to wet your whistle—got some pretty strong hooch out back."

"No thanks," Mac said. "Appreciate it, but we're on duty." He would have loved a cold drink of water after the long dusty ride but couldn't imagine drinking it out of what would probably be a filthy glass.

Fritz watched Harry approach the bookcase and stare at a picture on the top shelf. "Mind if I look at this?"

As he reached for the picture, Fritz rushed toward Harry, tripping over Mac's leg. "Let me get that for you."

"I got it, thanks." Harry looked at the picture. "Is this your daughter?" He handed the picture to Fritz.

"It's my wife and daughter. It's all I have left of them." He lowered himself onto a chair not taking his eyes from the picture. "Her mother just up and left me. Guess I weren't good enough for her. She thought she was so high and mighty."

"Strange she left her daughter behind. How old was Tracy when her mom left?"

"Hell, I don't know. She was just a kid and better off without that bitch."

Harry looked up at Mac, then gently took the picture out of Fritz's hand and studied it. "Your daughter was a beautiful girl. She looks like her mom."

"Yes, and believe me, I'm sick of hearing how much she looked like her mom. What about me? I didn't look so bad when I was young. You know, I played football some in school, could have played in my senior year if my ma didn't make me quit so I could help with the farm."

"This wedding picture—your mom and dad?"

Fritz squinted at the shelf. "Yep. My damn dad almost drank himself to death… You guys done with me yet? I'm tired and I still have some chores to finish before dark. This isn't the grand nursery it was a ways back, but I still sell shrubs and trees. And I still do all the planting myself. Yep, you can see my work all through town."

"What about it, Mac—you almost finished?"

"Just about. By the time you put the picture back, I'll be ready."

When Harry turned to put the picture back, Fritz yelled to be careful as he reached for the top shelf. It startled him and an old cigar box tumbled.

"Now look what you've gone and done!" Fritz screamed.

Harry caught the box before it hit the floor, but a few items fell out.

Fritz ripped the box out of his hand. "Damn it, they're mine."

Harry looked down at the things in his hand—mismatched earrings.

"I said, give them to me."

"Hold on." Harry took the box from Fritz and noticed the man's clenched fists as he did so. He lifted the lid and put the earrings in. "Here you go, nothing broken. Let me put these back."

"Give me my box. You better pray to God you didn't break nothin'. These here are family heirlooms. Why the pearl earrings in this box are the ones my wife is wearing in that picture. Yep, bought 'em myself…and these are my mom's…"

"I'm sorry for being so clumsy, Mr. Fritz. Mac, we should go and let this man get to his chores."

Mac shot Harry a surprised look. Then, in an instant, he stood and thanked Fritz for his time and trouble. The old man didn't say a word, just stood there holding the cigar box, glaring at Harry.

Harry picked up Mac's briefcase and hurried him toward the door. Fritz never moved as he watched them leave.

Mac stayed quiet until they got into the car. "Okay, what's going on here? That look you gave me would have killed a lesser man."

"You did good. You kept your cool. I wanted to get out of there without raising suspicion, but I don't think our act fooled the old man."

"What act?"

"Just drive until the car is out of view. We need to call for backup."

Mac did as he was told and as soon as they were far enough away, Harry put in the call. Mac waited patiently until he was finished.

"Damn, what a gruesome find." Harry rotated his head in a circular motion releasing tension. "Let's get out of the car and walk back towards the house. We'll keep an eye on him until help comes."

As Harry started walking, Mac grabbed his arm and spun him around. Harry pulled loose. "Easy, kid. Take your hands off me. I might be a little older, but you really don't want to mess with me."

"Then stop messing with me and tell me what the hell is going on. Did you see a corpse in that damn cigar box?"

Harry released a big breath rubbing his jaw. "Yeah, I did. In fact, I saw several."

"What the hell are you talking about?"

Harry continued to look hard at the house before turning to Mac. "Trophies."

Mac didn't miss the sad look in Harry's eyes. "Oh, God, no." Bile erupted in his throat as he put his head down with his hands on his knees.

Harry put his hand on Mac's back. "Come on, don't lose it now." He looked down the driveway toward the road. It was getting dark and cold. *Where the hell are you guys?*

A loud blast echoed through the still night. Resting birds in the nearby trees filled the air adding to the chaos. Mac and

Harry ran toward the house. As they got close, they saw a light in the barn.

"This way." Mac headed in that direction.

The pungent smell of gun smoke greeted them through a crack in the barn door, both men drew their guns. Harry pushed the door open—Fritz sat slumped over a bail of straw with a syrupy, red liquid dripping on the cigar box in his lap. In one hand he held a gun, in the other, the picture of his wife and daughter. As they looked at the gruesome sight, the picture fell to the ground next to Fritz.

Harry slowly put his gun away and blessed himself.

"Why the hell are you saying a prayer for that bastard!"

Harry lowered his head. "Mac, it's for the innocents at his feet."

Both turned as another loud blast broke the silence of the night. This time it was the wail of sirens.

Twenty-Four

Harry walked into Mac's office and parked himself on one corner of his desk. "Well, it looks like we had a serial killer living among us and we didn't have a friggin' clue."

Mac closed the file he had been studying. "Don't be so hard on yourself, Harry. Fritz was a recluse, lived 30 miles from nowhere. A stripe on a zebra no one noticed. Sad to say, the only friend that family seemed to have was Celeste."

"Yeah, Mac, but with all my training—why didn't I suspect him?"

"Because he was written off as a simple farmer who struggled to make a go of his land after his wife left him to raise a daughter. There was no indication he had trouble with his daughter. No, there's only one person to blame and that's Fritz.

"How about we wrap up some loose ends?"

Harry agreed. "Let's do it. You start."

"Well, I have several scenarios running through my head."

"Like what?"

"Say the girls were planning to run away together. Old Fritz heard them making plans—he admitted to eavesdropping before—and that meant he would lose his helper on the farm. God knows what else she was to him after his wife ran away."

"Hold on, Mac."

"Stick with me here. This is pure speculation. Let's say he *was* that kind of man and he hears Celeste talking Tracy into running away with her. He hears their plans to get enough money to make it to another city and he's furious. He confronts Tracy and Celeste. The three of them have a huge argument that gets out of hand. What do you think so far?"

"I'll play along. Then what?"

"The argument escalated and he ended up killing both girls."

Harry interrupted. "Timing isn't right. Celeste was seen after she was at his farm, wasn't she?"

"Can't remember. What about this: Old Fritz panics about losing Tracy. He lays the law down to both girls, but he can tell he's not getting anywhere with them. He lays awake nights trying to figure out what to do. It comes down to getting rid of Celeste permanently. He reckons Tracy will calm down after her friend is gone and things will get back to normal. He doesn't balk at killing Celeste. Then, he remembers the tennis court construction at Concord—the perfect place for Miss Adams. No one would ever find her.

"Now, I haven't pieced together what happened to Tracy yet, but considering the findings at the tennis court site, I'd say she and her dad had a knockdown drag out fight and she came out on the short end of the stick."

Harry flinched at the vision. "Mac, that's raw."

"Well, life is raw sometimes—you know that. Anyway, now he had another body to dispose of, so he used the same site. Let's face it, this man might have killed two girls. There is never a good excuse to kill. Looks like we'll never know the whole horrible story. I keep expecting our investigators to find Tracy alive somewhere far away from here. This hasn't gone down as I thought it would. I had Burton behind bars for whatever happened to Celeste."

"Yeah, I did too, Mac. Everything pointed to him, but there's always that question of guilt, isn't there?"

"What about the earrings in the box? His trophies? Harry, we could be talking serial killer."

"Could be,we should have a report any day now. If Fritz did away with the Milford girl and that's a big IF, it's terrifying what the earrings will tell."

"What's bad, if Fritz *is* the guilty party in the Milford case, we will probably never know what he did with her body."

"Mac, I'm afraid that old, decaying farm holds lots of secrets."

Twenty-Five

Mac had started to relax in his comfortable, oversized leather desk chair when Harry rushed in waving a paper and looking like he had discovered a gold mine.

"Man, oh man, oh man, have I got news for you."

"If it's good, lay it on me."

"It's good. Our man Fritz's dear old dad is alive and well in a nursing home over on Highway 640. Actually, I don't know how well he is, but he's alive."

Mac registered surprise. "You gotta be kidding. He'd have to be older than dirt. Fritz reportedly said that after his mother left him, daddy boy raised him until he was out of high school, and then he was nowhere just like the mother. Fritz indicated he was dead, didn't he?"

Harry smiled. "No, he said his old man *nearly* drank himself to death."

"Son of a bitch. You're right."

"That I am. I was going over the case with Joan—she took that one sentence, did some research, and found old man Fritz. Love that woman."

Mac smiled. "I see it every time you're together."

"Hell, didn't mean to say that."

"Yes you did."

"Get that smile off your face. Get focused. Instead of digging up those secrets at the farm, let's go dig around old man Fritz."

"You up for it?"

"Right behind you."

TWENTY-SIX

"Nice place," Mac said.

"Nice? C'mon. All I see is long, C-curved, white brick building."

"Get out. The name, Willow Resthaven, is welcoming, don't you think?" Not waiting for an answer, he went on, "And the vines covering the walls. My grandmother used to try to get those started on her house but never had any luck."

Harry laughed. "Know what I see? Green tentacles reaching out from the vines waiting for their next victim."

"Admit it," Mac countered. "Willow Resthaven is a tranquil substitute for home. You know, comfortable in a homespun kind of way."

"I don't have to admit anything." Harry frowned in a playful way. "Get on inside."

Mac opened the door to a peaceful entry with numerous cinnamon deodorizers strategically placed to overcome antiseptic odors.

A handsome, seventy-some year old woman with white hair manicured as finely as the front lawn greeted Mac and Harry. After she introduced herself as the manager, she offered assistance.

Harry spoke first, assuming a friendly conversational tone. "Mrs…" He scanned her suit jacket for a nametag.

She laughed, looking ten years younger. "It's Mrs. Cameron, but my husband has been gone many years." She winked at Harry. "So, if you want to have coffee sometime, I'm available."

"Well…"

"My dear man, don't look so worried. I'm kidding. Now, what can I do for you?"

Badges flashed.

"Oh, my. Is there a problem?"

Mac took her arm and maneuvered her into the closest office. "Please, don't be alarmed. We need to ask a few questions about one of your residents."

Mrs. Cameron's blue eyes widened. "Surely no one living here would do anything to require the police."

"No, no. We just need to talk to one of your residents."

"His name?"

"His last name is Fritz. Do you have a Mr. Fritz in residence?"

She pulled out the file drawer to the right of her desk. "Let me see. I know most of our residents. That name doesn't ring a bell, but my memory isn't as sharp as it used to be." As she thumbed through the files, Mac noticed her hands trembling.

"Mrs. Cameron, please don't be upset. This is a routine matter and nothing to worry about."

She forced a tight smile admitting she had never dealt with the police before and it was unnerving. "Hold on, now. Here it is, Lloyd Fritz."

"Can you tell us if Lloyd Fritz has a son named Ralph?"

"According to his file, Ralph is listed as his only living family member," she said.

"Is Lloyd Fritz still here?"

"Yes. I don't know why I didn't remember him when you asked. Fritz is an unusual name and I have to tell you he is quite an unusual man."

"In what way?"

Mrs. Cameron rose and shut the office door quietly. "Officers, anything we discuss stays confidential, doesn't it?"

"Of course. What do you want to tell us?"

Her eyes twinkled. "Well, he's a very mean old man."

"In what way, Mrs. Cameron?"

"He's quite old, you know. Let me check his birth date. Here it is. He's 97 and meaner than an angry herd of elephants."

"Mean? In what way?"

"Guess I should say he torments everyone—especially the ladies."

"Does his son visit him?"

"I don't remember him visiting and I've been here fifteen years. Wait, though, and I'll check his file." She turned to the visitor sheet. "No, it doesn't look like a son is signed in. There's always rumors floating around a retirement home—it keeps the folks occupied. I don't believe half of them, but in Mr. Fritz's case, maybe."

"Can you fill us in?"

Mrs. Cameron pulled a chair up beside Harry. "You know I kinda feel like that lady detective on TV—you know the one, the lady from Maine who solves all the crimes."

"You're talking about Angela Lansbury I imagine, but I'm afraid this isn't television—it's real life. Now, if you…"

"Of course, forgive me. There are some notations in the file that when he came here, he screamed and hollered about his wife leaving him and his boy. He told everyone who would listen that she was a…" her face reddened, "she was that B word."

"Mrs. Cameron, we hear that word more than you would believe. Go on, please."

"Like I said, he told anyone who would listen that his wife played around and he didn't even know if his son was really his. He said he doubted it, but he couldn't put him out on the street when his wife left—the boy was too young and he needed help around the farm."

"Nice man."

"Oh, not so nice, young man. Anyway, he obviously hates women and torments the ladies here. No one wants to sit by him in the eating area or in the game room. He's always coming on to the ladies and not in a discriminating way if you know what I mean."

"Is he well enough for us to see him?"

"Yes, I suppose he is for his ninety-seven years. I should warn you, though, that he becomes belligerent at the least little thing. Mention of either his wife or his son will set him off."

"If we set him off, I assume the medics will take over."

She laughed softly. "Of course. Can you tell me anything else about whatever it is you're investigating?"

Mac stood. "I'm afraid not, Mrs. Cameron. You know how we police are."

"Yes and I'm an investigator like Angela."

Harry took her hand and patted it gently. "You are indeed and you've been a big help. Now, can you have someone show us to Fritz's room?"

"I'll take you myself."

As they left the office, Father Andrew came through the front door.

"Andy, what in the world are you doing here?"

He grinned. "What in the world are *you* doing here, big brother? Hello, Mac. I don't know why my brother is surprised to see me—I'm just doing what a priest does."

Harry excused himself from Mrs. Cameron and Mac and pulled Andy to one side. "Isn't Willow Resthaven out of your area?"

"Right, I'm helping Father George today. He had a doctor's appointment. What the heck brings you here?"

"Paying a visit to Mr. Fritz."

"Fritz? Isn't that the name of the man you were investigating?"

"Yes, but this is his old man. Want to come along?"

"Lead the way. Mac won't mind, will he?"

"Don't worry about Mac. He'll be glad you're with us." He turned from his brother.

"Mrs. Cameron. Mac. Father Andy will come along if that's okay. Ready?"

The manager nodded and led the way to the left wing of the retirement home. When she stopped short of Room 1150, she turned to Mac and asked that he give her a few minutes to announce their visit.

While they waited outside the entrance, a shrieking voice

reverberated through the door. "I don't want any stinkin' visitors, old lady. I don't have anyone left but that worthless piece of shit some call my son and he never comes to see me."

"Calm down, Mr. Fritz. It's Father Andy. He's been by a time or two in Father George's place. You remember him, don't you?"

"Hell, no. What in hell's name do I want with a priest. I'm not dying, am I?"

"Of course not. Calm down or I'll have to call the medic."

After a few minutes of silence, Mac motioned Father Andy to approach the old man. Fritz sat with his back to the door.

"Good morning, Mr. Fritz, and how are we today?"

The old man wheeled his chair around with the strength of a younger man. He looked cramped in the wheelchair—obviously a tall man. He was gaunt with a full head of salt and pepper hair. The sun had reduced his withered, parchment like skin to an ugly tobacco brown. His red rimmed, milky blue eyes added to his menacing presence. It was clear he was a man to be reckoned with in his time.

"How do you think 'we are', young man? I'm in hell waiting for the devil to grab me by my gonads. You preach about hellfire, don't you?"

"Mr. Fritz, I try to keep people out of hell. You can get out if you want."

Lloyd Fritz spit on the floor. "Too late for me." He looked at Mac and Harry. "Who are those asses giving me the once-over?"

Mac extended his hand for a shake after he and Harry showed their badges and introduced themselves. Fritz returned their introductions with a crooked smile. "If you boys are trying to impress me, forget it. What in hell do you want?"

Mac started. "We want to ask about your son Ralph. When was the last time you saw him?"

"Dang if I know. If I did, I wouldn't tell you. My bastard son has been dead to me for years."

Mac and Harry exchanged looks.

"Well, Mr. Fritz, that's one reason we're here. Ralph *is* dead and we wanted to let you know."

"Good riddance."

"I doubt you mean that. We also wanted to ask about your wife."

"I'm not talking about that slut. She was no good, left me and the boy." He looked at Father Andy. "What do I call you?"

"Father or Andy is fine."

"All rightee, Andy. I'm not sure Ralph is my boy. His tramp of a mother played around on me. You know what that means?"

Father Andy smiled. "Of course I know what that means."

"Didn't know since you have that damned white collar choking you. Anyway, she went around with lots of men and I can't tell you to this day why I fell in love with her. She had somethin' all right and she showed it to everyone who looked." Fritz's face reddened.

"Calm down, sir. Getting excited isn't good for your heart."

Fritz made a sound imitating laughter. "Not good for my heart. You think I have a heart? Well, I don't—that whore stomped on what you're calling my heart and threw it away. She got what she deserved."

Harry's eyes sharpened. "What she deserved, sir? What was that?"

Fritz glared at them. "I tell you she got what she deserved. That son of mine, sniffling baby, I ruled him with an iron fist, that boy *never* disobeyed me, he knew better. Yep, he did what I told him to do…he watched. Yessiree, the damn woman ended up in hell and I could have danced."

"He watched?"

"That's right. He knew when someone disobeyed me, they got a whippin' and that included his mom. That day she got a good one. That put the fear of God in him." He hit his knee, "Yep, that day I did the whooping and he did the digging." The old man laughed so hard he choked.

Harry patted him on his back. "What did you say? You say she died?"

"What if I did? Good riddance. She was no good for the boy, whether he was mine or not, and she wasn't any good working the farm. She used to say that something, anything, had to be better than slaving in the dirt."

Fritz's eyes clouded like drapes had pulled across them. He wheeled the chair toward the window. Mac knew this was all they would get. He nodded to Harry and Father Andy to leave. Once outside, Mac asked, "What do you guys make of that disgusting filth spewing from his mouth?"

Harry hesitated shoving his hands deep in his pockets. He caught Father Andy's stare. "What do you think, little brother?"

Father Andrew touched the cross hanging around his neck. "I think Mr. Fritz could use an exorcism."

TWENTY-SEVEN

Mac spun around hearing a rap on his door. At the same time, his fax machine hummed, bringing the long awaited medical examiner's report. "Are you in cahoots with these good people, Harry?"

"If only." Harry grabbed the report from the machine and took a few seconds to pore over the results.

"Tell me what it says before I tear it out of your hand."

"See for yourself." He handed it to Mac

Mac read a moment then kicked the edge of his desk. "Damn. Short and sweet."

"They always are, I wonder sometimes if they realize how life altering these reports are. *Yes, this is the DNA of your loved one…so, they're dead, or no, keep looking.*

"Right… Okay, it says there was sufficient tissue on one pair of earrings for them to declare it a match to Pam Hornsby." He paused. "Thank God for the hair samples from her brush."

"You had more than that, didn't you?"

"Yeah, we got lucky." Mac frowned at Harry. "On the first sweep of Pam's room, we found some blood soaked bandages in her wastebasket. According to her parents, she had skinned her knees pretty bad in practice a few days before she disappeared."

"Back to the earrings a minute. You said there was tissue on them. What the hell did the madman do, tear them from her ears?"

"Looks like it. There's no telling what this son-of-a-gun has done."

Harry responded. "Okay, I remember a couple of pairs were tarnished, old looking, but the other ones looked trendier."

Mac laughed. "You're a fashion expert now?"

"Not hardly, smart ass."

"Sorry, Harry, just trying to lighten the mood."

"Yeah, keep reading."

Mac slapped the papers in his hand. "First of all, the DNA on a pair of the old silver ones matches Ralph Fritz's mother; secondly, from the wedding picture we have of his dad's folks, I'm damn sure the silver pearl ones were Ralph's grandmother's."

Harry hit the desk with his fist. "Holy hell. It appears that Lloyd Fritz killed his wife, Ralph's mother, and made his son sit and watch. But come on, his old man killed *his* mother? Little Ralphie's grandmother?"

"I'm as shocked as you, my friend. Sounds like something out of Shakespeare. Both their brains were twisted, decaying pieces of Grey matter. Too bad young Fritz blew his out, we could have father and son on trial. Think of the stories they could tell."

"Probably too much for anyone to bear. There are still five earrings unaccounted for. Lord, where are the poor souls they belong to?" Mac sat down and looked at Harry. "What do you think the DA will do with old man Fritz, Mac?"

"I'd like to see them drag the old devil out of that nursing home and throw him in jail. He doesn't deserve a trial. Those rotten bastards destroyed so many innocents. And who knows how long this madness lived in their family…how many generations? Harry, think of it…that old farm might be a mass grave site."

Twenty-Eight

Mac collected all the files pertinent to the Adams' case and reviewed his list of things to do. He hadn't called Lillian with an update. As he picked up his cell, it vibrated in his hand.

"Hey. Lillian. Great minds work alike. I was just going to call you. Tell me something good."

Lillian laughed softly. "Well, death is never good, but..."

"You're helping us find a killer, Lillian and that's good. Anyway, what's up?"

"The puzzle is fitting together. I'd like you to come by the lab."

"Finished with the reconstruction?"

"Not completely, but enough to give you a pretty good visual."

"Good. Wait until you hear what we have to tell you."

"You sound pretty excited. I hope this reconstruction completes your puzzle."

When Mac and Harry walked into the lab, they froze.

Harry blessed himself. "Jesus, Mary and Joseph."

Lillian looks startled. "Harry, what?"

"It's Tracy Fritz, Celeste's friend. Damn, Fritz did kill his own daughter."

"Dear God."

Mac spoke up. "Damn, Lil, you are dead-on, excuse the pun. This is definitely a big piece of the puzzle. Sad, this beautiful young girl has to be part of such an ugly puzzle."

"Obviously you guys hit pay dirt. Looks like my work is finished here. It's late, I'm tired and hungry. Let's go to the restaurant around the corner—I want to hear your story."

As soon as they settled around a table and ordered drinks, Lillian listened in awe and disgust. "You know, I have been around for quite a few years—this is some tale you're weaving." She sipped her wine before putting her glass on the table. She looked at Harry and Mac. "You found yourself a f'n serial killer."

She hesitated as the men exchanged looks.

Mac blew air between his pinched lips and Harry shook his head. "That's right. Geez, Lil, how do you handle this work?"

"Because it's rewarding. Look what our team…"

"Team?"

"Yes. Look what you, Harry, and I have done for these victims and their families. We've given them closure, albeit a sad one. Bottom line, my work is an act of love and I can see the results."

"Gotcha."

"Guys, I'm proud you made me part of your crew."

"What would we have done without you?"

The three raised their glasses. Lillian smiled. "Mac, my report will be on your desk tomorrow and I guess this is good-bye."

Mac gave her a wicked grin. "Not if I have anything to say about it."

Twenty-Nine

A surge of relief spread through Mac. He was close to putting Celeste's memory to rest. He had agonized all these years over Celeste. He had compared every woman he met to her. He froze his memories in time and only let them thaw slightly when he met new women. Then he would imagine how Celeste would be if she had lived and the other women never compared.

Mac shook his head. *What in hell would a psychiatrist say about me?*

The phone buzzed and an officer announced two men were there to see him. The young cop said one of the men was an attorney by the name of George Smithers. When Mac approached the front desk, he was surprised to see Ted Burton. Smithers lost no time introducing himself as Burton's attorney asking if Mac could give them a few minutes.

He ushered them into one of the interview rooms. Mac ignored Burton's icy glare keeping his focus on Smithers. "Have a seat, gentlemen. What can I do for you?"

Burton couldn't keep his temper in check. "You sonofabitch, you can leave…"

Smithers interrupted. "Officer Hudson, my client tells me you came by Concord recently and talked to him about Celeste Adams. Is he a suspect in this girl's disappearance?"

Mac frowned—he didn't like admitting he was wrong. "He is not a suspect at this time, Mr. Smithers."

Burton's face reddened. "Then why in the name of God did

you come by the school harassing me?"

Mac ignored him never taking his eyes from the attorney. "There was no harassment. If your client thinks otherwise, I'm sorry. We pursued Mr. Burton as a person of interest. That's all there was to it."

Burton interrupted again. "I want you to leave me alone. Do you understand?"

"Mr. Smithers, please advise your client there was no harassment, and if he leads a clean life, why would he be worried?"

Smithers stood and held Burton's arm. "I think our business is concluded. We thank you for your time." He extended a business card. "If you have any further interest in Mr. Burton, please contact me direct."

Burton pulled out of his grasp and swung at Mac. "I told you I was innocent, you sonofabitch."

Mac smiled. He had infuriated Burton and that was what he wanted. So, Teddy felt watched and annoyed. Good. Mac knew in his heart that even though Burton hadn't killed Celeste, he had damaged her. One thing wouldn't change for Burton, he would continue to be the champion of the football team, one of Concord's greats.

Mac had to close the book on Burton, get him out of his head, and let the chips fall where they may.

THIRTY

The next morning Mac Hudson and Harry O'Donnell gathered in Mac's office. They stared at each other in silence. It was time—time to talk to the Adams family—time to complete Celeste Adams' journey. Harry called Father Andy and the family asking them to meet in St. Vincent's chapel.

Father Andy sat alone in the chapel, his eyes wandered to the candles burning in front of the altar—they filled the small area with a warm glow. He felt at peace and prayed that he, along with Mac and Harry, could convey this feeling to the family. Footsteps startled him. He turned to see Harry, Joan, and Mac coming in. They nodded and sat beside him.

"Little brother, the time has come. Are you ready for this?"

"Never ready, Harry. Not for something like this."

Celeste's parents came in, accompanied by Michael and Rachel.

Harry spoke quietly to the family, empowered by Father Andy and the surroundings. He explained what they had found and that there had been a positive identification. Quiet murmurs of sadness mixed with tears of loss filled the chapel.

Jim Adams stood to express his and his family's gratitude to Mac and Harry. He looked at Father Andy with a sad smile.

"How could Fritz's instability go unnoticed? It's shocking. You know, Celeste was at his farm so often, I'm surprised she didn't pick up on his craziness. If we had kept her away from Fritz's farm…well, maybe she would be with us—"

"Don't think that way," Harry interjected. "How could you, or anyone else, know any of this at the time?"

As Jim went to take his seat, Michael motioned toward the vestibule. Then, he leaned over to Mac whispering, "How about a few words in the entry area?"

Once together, Mike looked at his father. "Dad, I know you want to hear more about Burton."

"You got that right, son. So, Mac, what about Burton? How could we be so wrong about the man?"

"Everything pointed to him. We were just following a trail. By the way, Burton and his attorney came to the precinct a few days ago."

Michael and his dad both reacted. "You're kidding."

"No. He accused me of harassing him."

"So, he hired an attorney?"

"Yep. He seemed like an all right guy."

"But, Burton..."

"Mike, we need to forget about Burton. He's been in our heads way too long. Let's get back to the chapel—I think Father Andy is ready to offer Mass."

Mike grabbed Mac's sleeve. "Hold on. We want to thank you again for what you've done here. Without you and Harry, my family might never have known what happened to Celeste. We are so grateful."

"No need for thanks, Mike. A lot of people have been involved in solving your sister's case. As far as Harry and I are concerned, this is what we do, although it's been especially hard because it was so personal."

"It was a long time before we realized you had a relationship with Celeste."

Mac smiled. "I wish I could call it a relationship, but it was only a friendship—a special one for me." Tears gathered in his eyes. "Jim, your daughter, and Mike, your sister, was very kind and took me under her wing. I'm glad she can rest now."

THIRTY-ONE

Father Andy walked into his office and looked at his desk littered with papers. It had been a long and emotional day with those close to Celeste Adams. The pale shades of lavender and pink shimmering through the leaded glass window told him the sun was setting. He sat, leaned back in his chair, and enjoyed what was left of the daylight. As the room's golden glow faded, he turned on the desk lamp. Rachel was due soon. He was eager to finish the research he promised her. Even though they had picked out some of her mother's most beautiful photos for the exhibition, the ones she took in Cairo continued to pique his interest.

He scanned the papers. According to reports, the first apparition was seen over the Coptic Orthodox Church of Saint Mary at Zeitoun on the night of April 2, 1968. This apparition was witnessed by two Muslim watchmen. They informed authorities they were afraid the woman was going to jump. They shouted. A crowd gathered. After that, the nightly apparitions were seen by millions of Egyptians and foreigners, including people of various faiths—Eastern Orthodox, Roman Catholics, Protestants, Muslims, Jews, as well as those with no particular belief systems.

It wasn't long before newspapers reported the extraordinary sightings—*Progres Dimanche*, the Egyptian French weekly, published news of the apparition on their front page, May 5, 1968. *The New York Times* added their report of the story on the same day. A year later, April 11, 1969, *The Egyptian Gazette's* headline read, "Apparition of Virgin Still Being Seen."

According to news reports, most of the people who either saw the apparitions or read the stories believed it was the Blessed Mother or an Egyptian Goddess—some even insisted it was a hoax.

Father Andy contemplated the photographs taken at Zeitoun again. He couldn't believe he was viewing photos taken at the actual time of the apparitions. He had, of course, heard about these sightings, but this was the first time he realized pictures were taken by various reporters confirming the same image.

There's no doubt something or someone is in the photographs. If it's you, Blessed Mother, what are you trying to say? What can I do as a man of Faith? I do believe, but as I get older and time goes on, the water gets muddier.

What's Rachel's message? She witnessed the miracle with her mom and has pictures to prove it. Actually, when I think about it, Rachel has been involved in two miracles that have been in the public eye.

Dear God, is this world in such bad shape that the deities feel the need to make the nightly news?

Andy jumped when the door to his study opened.

Rachel waved. "Sorry, Father, didn't mean to startle you. Mattie sent me in. Did I wake you?"

He shook his head. "Don't think so. I don't know, Rachel. I was lost in thought. Sorry I'm in such a fog—my manners seem to be floating out there too. Let me help you with your package." As he took it from her hands, the cover fell off.

"Holy Mother, look at this!" He held it closer to the light. "A picture of the apparition, Rach. This one even has the doves in the background. Man, it looks good framed."

"I'm glad you like it. It's a gift for all your help."

"What? No way. I can't accept this—it's too much."

"Yes, you can. I can't think of a better place for this photo to be than here with you. Please, Father Andy, you have done so much for us."

He carefully laid the picture on his desk and wrapped his arms around Rachel.

"Thank you, dear friend. I will cherish it." Father heard the door open again. He turned to see the housekeeper.

"Well, that doesn't look like work to me," Mattie said as she brought in a tray of coffee and scones.

"Oh, go on, I'm just thanking Rachel for this unbelievable gift."

Mattie set the tray by the window and walked over to look closer at the picture. "So this is one of the photographs you've been telling me about." She continued to gaze at it as she slowly ran her fingers over its surface. She looked at Rachel and Father Andy with tears in her eyes. "It's so lovely, yet so sad."

"Sad, Mattie? Why?"

"Because she keeps coming back and no one cares. She let herself be heard and seen by children. This time she showed herself to millions. Why? You'd think she would give up on us." Mattie used her apron to wipe away marks on the glass. She shook her head and blessed herself.

"We care, Mattie."

"I know dear." Mattie patted Father Andy's arm. "I know." She slowly walked to the door, then turned. "Goodnight, you two, and, Father, don't forget you have an early mass in the morning."

They watched the door close behind the housekeeper.

Father Andy broke the silence. "That's an interesting concept."

"Right! Why keep trying to save us when we keep screwing up?" Andy looked at her and raised one eyebrow.

"You don't have to give me that look. I know how blessed I am, and I know mothers should never give up on their children, but there's so many unanswered questions out there." She sighed as she collapsed in a chair.

"Don't I know it?" He closed his eyes and whispered. "A mother should never give up on her children...she's trying to save us..."

"What did you say, Father?"

"Just thinking aloud, Rachel. You know, I'm too tired to get into the Meaning of Life tonight. Let's have some coffee and get to work."

Rachel looked at herself in the mirror, happy with her decision to wear the blue cashmere suit. She was brushing her long blonde hair when Michael walked in.

"Whoa, girl, you look stunning. Where do you think you're going looking like that...and without me?"

She smiled and gave him a kiss. "Thanks for the compliment. I want to make a good impression on Vincent Grey."

"Believe me, you will." Michael leaned on the door-jamb, blocking her way. "And just who is this Mister Vincent Grey?"

"Let's see, he's tall, dark and gorgeous, in his early thirties I'd say, very sexy." She winked. "Oh, yeah, he's extremely wealthy."

Michael drummed his fingers on the door. "Rachel, I'm not finding this the least bit funny."

She moved close to him trailing her fingers down his arms. "Really? I'm having fun. Are you going to keep me from seeing him?"

Michael gripped her wrist. "Enough with the teasing and you know better than to call my bluff. I have a meeting to go to, but I can make both of us very, very late." He kissed her, holding her close.

"Tempting..."

"Rach!"

"All right. Vincent Grey is the owner of the Grey Gallery in that new Loft building downtown." Not getting a response, she continued. "Hellooo, my mom's exhibit?"

"Oh, *that* Vincent Grey. I knew all along—just giving you a hard time."

"Liar!"

"Okay, now that we have that settled, let's get out of here. We're both going to be late."

Rachel started down the hall but stopped when she heard Michael say, "Rach, love you."

She turned and threw him a kiss.

Rachel thanked God she found a parking place close to Grey's Gallery. She hurried down the street, checking her watch—not too late. She pushed the gallery door to enter at the same time someone opened it from the other side. She fell into Father Andy's arms at the precise moment Vincent Grey entered from the back room.

Grey strode toward them with his hand extended. "Hello, Rachel, and this handsome gentleman must be Michael."

Rachel untangled herself from Father Andy.

"Sorry," Rachel stuttered. "This is a dear friend, Father Andy. I asked him to meet me here because he's been helping with the exhibit."

Grey eyed Father Andy up and down. "Father, you say. You're a priest?"

Andy put his hand out to shake. "Uh, yes. You see, I don't always wear my collar." He looked sheepishly at Rachel.

"Interesting." Grey shook Andy's hand, then acknowledged Rachel with a kiss on her cheek. "I would prefer to call you Father Andrew, if that's all right."

"Of course."

"And, please—my friends call me Grey. Now that we have all that out of the way, let's get this tour started." He clapped his hands and two assistants appeared out of nowhere. They fawned over Rachel and Andy giving them flutes of champagne and offering various edibles. As they walked and talked, the assistants constantly scribbled notes, glancing at Grey constantly for approval.

Grey appeared unaware of his assistants' nervousness.

"Rachel, I can't tell you how happy I am that you chose my gallery to exhibit Margaret Benson's work. Your mother's photographs have been recognized and loved all over the world. It is truly an honor and I will make sure this is one showing no one will ever forget."

Rachel beamed with pride and took Grey's hands. *Lord, he is tall, dark and handsome.* "Thank you. Your studio is wonderful. I love the openness with all the glass and exposed steel."

"My father will be pleased—he designed it. Tell me, Andrew— oops, Father Andrew, do you like the idea of having the libations set up on the balcony so as not to interfere with the showing, and what do you think of having the walls painted black to make the photos pop?"

Andy put his hand on his chin as he scanned the area. "I'd say you're right on. I wouldn't want the libations anywhere else and we must have the photos pop!"

"Excellent. Now I'm feeling the love."

They both smiled and nodded enthusiastically.

Grey rubbed his hands together. "I'm so excited. Come on you two—say something."

Rachel walked up and hugged him. "I am speechless. I love it all. Grey, you've been so kind and put so much thought in every detail—food, drink, flowers, music."

"Oh, my dear, it's my pleasure." He motioned to Andy. "Come on over here, guy, and give us a hug." He turned to Rachel and winked as Andy walked over to them. He slapped Andy on his back and shook his hand.

"So, you really are a priest? Hmm, it has to be tough to have such an intoxicating friend as Rachel and stay in grace."

Andy cocked his head, pulled himself up to his full height, and looked Grey in the eye. "It's what makes my calling so interesting. I've always loved a challenge."

Grey smiled. "Good answer. I'll see you in church then."

Laughing, Grey turned to Rachel. "You two run along now. I have loads of work to do."

Once outside, they both giggled. Andy spoke first. "Whew, that was something. Mister Vincent Grey is quite a character."

"Yes, he is. Don't you love him, Father?"

Andy grinned. "Maybe not love, but he is very likable."

Rachel went to bed excited and full of anticipation. Sleep

came fast and morning too soon. When she opened her eyes, her dream was just a wisp of a shadow. She lay still and closed her eyes again trying to summon the dream again—her mother smiling and hugging her. The scent of her perfume Evening in Paris lingered. She didn't want to lose the total joy she felt in her dream, all was well with the world, and she was safe in her mom's arms.

"Rachel, honey, it's time to get up. We have a big day ahead of us."

She moaned and turned the other direction. "Go away. I'm in a happy place."

"Come on, baby. This is an important day for you and your mom."

Rachel's eyes shot open as she sat up. "Oh, my God, Michael, the exhibition."

He sat down on the bed and folded her in his arms. "That's right. I know you're exhausted, but we still have a lot to do."

She fell back, putting a pillow over her head.

THIRTY-TWO

The night was cold and crisp. A full moon filtered through the glass in the gallery. Rachel arrived early. As she walked in, she noticed Grey had placed flowers around the studio. The flowers filled the air with their fragrance. Lights were dim; she could hear voices in the distance, and bell-like sounds of glasses and plates being arranged. She took a deep breath as she enjoyed the beauty around her. She whispered, "Mom, this is your night."

Sensing someone in the shadows, Rachel turned. A man walked slowly toward her. Once he was close enough that she could feel his touch, he spoke in low tones. "Sorry, Rachel, I didn't mean to startle you. I wanted to give you a private moment."

Rachel reacted with as much calm as she could muster. "No need to apologize, Grey. I was caught up in the beauty of the gallery. Everything looks perfect."

He moved a few steps away. "My dear, wait until you see it when the lights go up."

Rachel turned as Michael, Mac, Harry, and Father Andy entered. She greeted Michael with a kiss as Andy took care of the introductions.

"Ah, Father Andrew. Good to see you again." Grey shook hands with Mac while scrutinizing Harry. "There's no mistaking you two are related. Harry, a pleasure to meet you. Your brother is an inspiration to me."

"Really? How so?"

"I admire his extreme dedication to his calling."

Andy laughed and shook his head.

Grey excused himself as Rachel and Michael approached. "I have some final preparations to attend to. Please get some champagne at the bar and relax while you can. It's going to be a night to remember."

Rachel admired Grey skating from one activity to another as smoothly as on ice. She heard some activity at the entrance. She caught Grey's eye and motioned him to take care of greeting the guest.

"Myra," Grey said in a low tone. "I'm glad you came early. Come meet Margaret Benson's daughter, her husband and friends."

Rachel watched as Grey escorted the new guest toward her. She was intrigued with this beautiful woman—long black hair and eyes to match. Her golden tan was intensified by her disarming smile. Her dress, a brilliant shade of turquoise, was enhanced by elegant gold jewelry.

"Close your mouths, men," Rachel murmured, "You're drooling."

After Grey made the introductions, he asked if they would tend to her until he got back.

Myra assured Grey and the group in a voice shaded with foreign tones that she was fine on her own but would love their company if they didn't mind.

"It's such a pleasure to meet Margaret Benson's daughter. I have admired your mother's work for a long time." She turned toward the men. "Gentlemen, it's a pleasure to meet all of you too. This is a night filled with promise. My mother was in Cairo the same time you and your mother were there, Rachel. In fact, she was pregnant with me at the time. She died a few years ago—she would have loved to have been here tonight. She spoke so highly of your mother's work—her favorites were the apparition photos. I plan to purchase one tonight."

As they talked, the gallery filled with people.

Andy leaned against a steel beam with a drink in his hand. He smiled to himself as he watched Rachel and Myra talking.

Silently Grey came up behind him and whispered.

"They are lovely wouldn't you agree, Father Andrew?"

Andy turned slowly. "I would indeed."

"And tempting?"

Andy glared at Grey.

"What is it, Andrew?" Grey patted the top of his head. "Do you see horns or a halo?"

"I haven't made up my mind yet."

"Come on. Holy men like you always know—that's what keeps you in grace and protects you." He winked and walked away.

Harry approached Andy. "You were right about that Grey fellow—he's a strange one. I don't know what to make of him."

"You don't have to make anything of him. I have him all figured out."

They turned at the sound of the bell indicating another sale. Rachel snuggled close to Michael. "I love that sound, Mike, and the night is only half over. I need to walk around and check, but I swear most of Mom's photos are sold."

"I think you're right. This calls for another glass of champagne."

Michael took her hand and walked toward the balcony, acknowledging friends and family as they went.

"Rach, I'm impressed with the large turnout. I knew your mom was well-known, but I swear we have the United Nations represented here tonight."

She looked around the room as they ascended the steps to the bar. "You're right and look toward the entrance—Myra is entertaining her own foreign entourage."

Michael leaned on the railing and looked down on the room. "Yes, she introduced them all to me at one point or another this evening. Even though they're scattered from parts unknown, they seem to be really good friends."

"Hey you two. People watching?"

"Father Andy." Rachel gave him a hug. "Yes we are and we're intrigued by Myra's friends."

"Hmm, intriguing is a good word for them. They have very interesting stories to tell."

"Excuse me? You know them, Andy?"

"I do and don't give me that look, Rachel. They only arrived a day or two ago, and things have been so hectic I haven't had a chance to talk to you."

Rachel turned to Michael. "Do you know what he's talking about?"

"No clue," Michael said smiling at Andy. "I did, however, find it strange that when I met them they knew all about us and my radio show."

"Well Michael, I guess that proves it, you really are a celebrity." Rachael said as she kissed him on the cheek.

The lights dimmed and Rachel heard Grey requesting she join him. She took Michael and Andy's hands and started down the steps. All of a sudden a spotlight flashed on. It followed them to Grey. Applause filled the room. Michael and Andy dropped back so Rachel would have the crowd's full attention.

Rachel's long flowing copper gown glistened in the lights. She wore her hair up with amber colored stones holding it in place. Grey held out his hand and kissed her on the cheek. "You are a vision of beauty tonight, Rachel."

The applause was overwhelming. Rachel felt her stomach twitch. She said a prayer she could stay calm. Grey held up his hands to silence the crowd.

"Thank you. Thank you for making this a magical night and welcome once again to Grey's Gallery. I told Rachel this would be a special night and from the comments I've heard, I believe you all agree."

Applause thundered through the gallery.

"Tonight we honor an extremely talented woman, Margaret Benson. When you look at Margaret's photographs, you see she had the ability to capture the soul of her subject. She also had the uncanny ability to be at the right place at the right time. Whether it was a terrible disaster or a miraculous vision, she was there to capture the heartbreak, or wonderment, for all to see. Some of you had the fortunate pleasure of knowing Margaret. Others, like myself, consider it a blessing to view and maybe own one of her masterpieces. I am so pleased to announce that all of Margaret Benson's photos in the Gallery have been purchased tonight. Thanks to your generosity, her daughter, Rachel, will present a check in Margaret Benson's memory to St. Clair Hospital in the amount of three million dollars for a new children's wing."

Oohs and ahhs spread throughout the studio followed by applause. Grey embraced Rachel then handed her the microphone.

Tears filled her eyes as she cleared her throat. Michael walked to her side, put his arm around her waist, and kissed her cheek before positioning himself behind her. Rachel pivoted to look at her children and Michael's parents. She composed herself and beamed at the crowd.

"I am overwhelmed by your kindness and generosity. I know my mother is here in spirit and filled with joy, as I am, to be among so many of her friends. You have made a wish of my mom's—a wish I neglected for too long—finally come true. I will be forever grateful. Thank you."

It took over an hour for the gathering to thin. Rachel asked Michael to send the kids home with his parents not knowing what time they could break away.

Father Andy scanned the crowd for his housekeeper and saw Mattie deep in conversation with some of Myra's friends.

"Mattie dear, it's very late. I thought you left with Michael's parents."

"Oh no, Father. I'm staying for a while. I have years to catch up with Brigid and Aonghus."

"Dear me, my sainted mom taught me better. Father, these are my dear friends."

"Mattie, no need to bring in your sainted mother. We've met. Myra introduced them to me earlier this evening." He acknowledged her friends and couldn't help notice their dress. Aonghus was wearing a kilt and Brigid a dress of the same plaid but covered with a beautiful hooded cape.

Father Andy noticed Harry, Michael, Rachel, and Grey heading his way after telling Mattie she could ride home with him.

"Ah, just the man we're looking for," Grey said. "I need a head count. My chef is preparing a light breakfast for friends and family that will be attending our meeting. I didn't realize it was so late."

Michael turned bewildered. "A meeting? Rachel and I weren't told about a meeting."

"I'm sorry. I assumed Father Andrew informed you." He turned toward Father Andy. "Should we do this in the morning?"

"Most of the group has flights out tomorrow. I know we're all tired, but breakfast will renew our energy. "Rach, Mike, please forgive me. So much has been going on, I haven't had time to talk to you about the meeting."

Grey grinned. "Too much to do, Father? I understand. Okay, I'll get things started and you play catch up with Michael and Rachel."

"What's going on, Andy? This has been such a spectacular night for our family and friends, but I'm getting concerned. What are we getting ourselves involved in?"

"Not to worry. I should have made time to explain all this, but it happened so fast. It started when I got involved in the research for the photos taken in Zeitoun. I heard about a priest, Father Boulos, a Coptic Bishop that was supposed to be a good source of information on the apparition. He told me there was a community called Patrons of Protection and put me in touch with a few members."

Michael gave his wife an anxious look. "Patrons of Protection? Is this some kind of cult?"

"No, not the way you mean it. This community has opened up doors I never knew existed. It's important for you two to get to know these people. It will give you a better understanding of what's happened this past year. Please, you're family. Trust me,

go in and listen with an open heart. Rachel, your mom belonged
to this Community."

Michael shot Rachel a surprised look.

"Andy, you have my head spinning. Rach and I do trust you.
We'll go to the meeting if it means so much to you. Besides, it's
late and breakfast sounds and smells good."

"Great, I'll get everyone together. Grey's holding the meeting in his conference room."

"Wait a minute. Don't tell us Grey is a member!"

"He is, and so is his dad. I believe his dad thinks he designed
and built the Gallery with this particular show in mind."

"What?"

"Believe me, it gets stranger. I just found out Mattie has friends
here. Look, here comes Bob. Do you two want him to stay?"

"I'd like to ask Harry and Mac to attend too, if that's okay."

"Of course, Father."

"Hey, guys. What's going on?" Bob eyed them. "You look
very suspicious."

They grinned, circling around him.

"Okay, mysterious ones. I want to say goodnight and thank
you for the invite." He hugged Rachel and shook Michael and
Andy's hands.

"Hold on, Bob, I'd like you to stay for a while." Michael said.

"What's up?"

"Some of the guests are holding a meeting of sorts, and want
us to attend. Father Andy assures us it will be quite interesting."

"Sure, Michael, if you want me too. Is that beautiful thing in
the turquoise dress staying?"

Michael glanced at Andy. "Yes, I think she might be the leader
of the Patrons of Protection."

Father Andy spoke up. "Bob, not to worry. I think you will
enjoy the meeting."

"What kind of meeting, Father? Wait, don't tell me—it has
something to do with those apparition pictures, right? You
know it takes very little to spook me. I mean I found the photos

interesting, ghosts and all but… Ah, come on guys, this past year has been one weird thing after another. Okay, not just weird—very sad, with the shootings and all."

"Stop rambling, Bob, it's going to be all right. I won't let anything happen to you."

Harry walked up with Mac. "What's so funny?"

Father Andy gave Harry a thumbs-up. "Listen, I have to get back to Grey. Can I count on all of you to come to the meeting?"

"You bet," Bob said. "I'll explain it to Harry and Mac."

Andy waved as he went in search of Grey.

"Hmm, count us in for what, Bob?"

Michael and Rachel nodded at him, "Go on, tell them."

"It has something to do with those ghost pictures Rachel's mom took. They want to have a meeting about them. I thought it would be a good idea if the law were present."

Harry enjoyed a deep belly laugh. "Ghost pictures—that's hilarious. Oh, I wouldn't miss this for the world. How about you, Mac?"

"I'm with you."

The lights in the gallery dimmed once again. The fragrance of fresh coffee and sounds of mingled voices lured them down a long hallway where they saw Father Andy leading a group.

As they walked, Michael whispered to Bob, "As soon as I have a chance, I'll introduce you to Myra." Bob showed surprise. "You know, buddy—the lady in turquoise."

"I think I'll pass." Bob winced. "Who knows what kind of hocus pocus she's into."

Michael slapped Bob on his back, "Man, you're good for the soul."

Rachel surveyed the meeting room, a massive chamber highlighted by an oval table of black marble surrounded by comfortable looking high-back chairs—a sharp contrast from the steel and glass of the gallery. The floor and two walls were lined with bookshelves finished in a rich, dark wood. The remaining walls were painted sunset gold. A large, ornate fireplace graced the back wall. A welcome blaze flickered there.

A tall, bewitching woman seemed to float toward Rachel. "Welcome dear, I'm Anca Dragos. I came all the way from Romania to see you and honor your mother." She spoke with a heavy accent. She took Rachel's hands. "My dear, your hands are so cold." She rubbed them. "There, there now, don't be nervous. Consider us family."

Rachel looked into the greenest eyes she had ever seen. Anca's silver white hair was captured in a snood encrusted with pearls. She wore a pewter satin jacket over a long, slim skirt. Rachel noticed she had a ring on every finger and a silver necklace dripping with crystal moons and stars encircled her neck.

Anca continued holding her hands and smiling. "Your mother was a very dear friend of mine. My dear, your eyes are sad. This is not a day for sadness. Please, take that husband of yours and mingle with your guests. Listen to their stories. I think you have much in common. You might remember some of them from your travels with your mom. They are eager to visit with you and Michael."

The moon dipped low in the sky. Rachel and Michael were immersed in conversation when Anca touched her shoulder. "Gather your friends and come sit by me. We must get started— the hour is late."

Rachel and Michael motioned for their friends to join them. Bob stayed close to Harry and Mac. Mike carried coffee and a plate of food to share with Rachel. She surveyed the room to locate Andy and found him sitting next to Grey and Myra. Soon all were seated. They ate and talked in quiet murmurs. When everyone seemed satisfied, the table was cleared, lights lowered, and candles lit. Anca stood and raised her hands. A hush fell over the group.

"Please join me in a blessing.
Golden flame of light and illumination
Fill our souls with liberation

CC Smith & Betty Gordon209

Release the love that we hold
So our destiny we can mold
May divine grace give us the sight
To save our world from its plight."

Anca slowly lowered her hands and addressed the group. "Friends, new and old, I want to thank you for coming. Some of you have traveled many miles to be here tonight because you heard the call of the Mother. It has been a long time in coming but she has brought us another glimmer of salvation. Oh, we are a strange mixture from all parts of the world. As I look around the room, I see followers of Brigid, from the Celtic Empire, Blessed Mother Mary, Tara, Kuan Yin, Lakshmi. As we all know, the Mother goes by many names be it Tibetan, Christian, Buddhist, Egyptian or Hindu. We all follow the Mother in our own way and faith. We know Our Mother has been pleading for humanity to find love and peace for many, many years.

"I had hoped like so many of you that I would see the miracle of peace in my lifetime. But the years fly by me like shooting stars. Now I am old and there is still evil among us. To my horror, the Mother's voice grows weak as evil grows stronger. I want all of you to know—seeing you here tonight and knowing that we are doing our best to accomplish our mission as Protectors makes this old heart glad. I know what I am saying sounds like riddles to our new friends, so now let me speak to them."

Bob took a gulp of his coffee and hit Harry in the ribs, "Oh God, I think she means us."

"Quiet, friend, listen," Harry whispered.

Anca turned to Rachel and Michael. "My dear children, you have been initiated into our order without even knowing it. You see, we are always watching and listening. Several of our members are big fans of your radio show, Michael.

"Don't look so surprised. We admire your constant vigilance where children are concerned. That's one of the reasons we believe the Mother picked you—the other is, of course, Rachel. While listening one night, they heard the mesmerizing voice of the woman you called Celeste. Some of them knew immediately. Others waited, and when your miracle happened, word spread throughout the Community. We were overjoyed. Hearing the Mother, knowing She has not lost faith in us was very comforting. I'm sure you and your friends have many questions for us, Michael. I have said enough."

As if on cue, Grey came over and escorted Anca to a chair by the fireplace and took a seat next to her.

Rachel and Michael sat in stunned silence. After a few minutes Rachel patted Michael's arm, stood and walked to the podium. She cleared her throat.

"I feel honored to be in your presence on this memorable night," Rachel said. "What Anca revealed tonight, I must confess I've kept suppressed for many years. As a young child, it was a fairy tale, as a teenager, I was too belligerent to care. Then, as a woman planning marriage and children, it went back to being just a fairy tale. I heard the caller on my husband's radio show that he named Celeste. I listened to her pleas. Never quite sure— but when I looked into the eyes of that woman as she saved my son's life, all my mom's teachings came back. I knew instantly who she was and that she was giving me and my son the most precious gift—life. It shook me to my core, but it also brought me great comfort. I was looking into the lens of my mom's camera— she was focusing it for me—loose threads of my life were being bound together. I felt whole. I want to thank you for sharing you friendship and your amazing stories with us this evening. Some of these stories go back generations—they are what binds us together—faith, love and hope.

"My story starts today, and I pray it spreads like branches on a tree for all the world to know that we were given a gift, we heard a plea, and we will never forget." All the unshed tears she'd kept hidden this past year fell with relief down her cheeks.

A rustling of chairs brought old and new friends to her side. The first one was Michael and within seconds they were folded in each other's loving arms.

Father Andy walked over to where Harry, Bob and Mac were sitting.

Harry looked up and patted a chair. "Have a seat little brother. This is turning out to be, to quote Grey, 'a night to remember.' What do you make of all this?"

Bob and Mac leaned in close, never taking their eyes off Andy.

"Yeah, Father Andy, what the hell? Excuse me, I mean, what the heck? Evidently Anca thinks this Celeste woman from Michael's show is some goddess or something." Bob was practically shouting as Michael and Rachel approached.

"Thank God. Michael, Rachel, come sit with us, we need to talk. I can't get my head wrapped around any of this."

"I know Bob, same here." Michael pulled chairs over so they could face each other. They all got comfortable before focusing their attention on Father Andy.

Harry pointed at his brother. "Looks like you're the man of the hour, Andy. You up for answering questions?"

"If I can, of course. You must understand though that I've been privy to this information for only the last week. I might add that since I'm a man of the cloth, it has had a major effect on me. Actually, Rachel is the one who should take your questions. That okay with you, Rach?"

"Sure, but what Anca said pretty much sums it up."

Michael shifted in his chair. "It sure as hell doesn't sum up this Celeste woman for me. Come on, I'm supposed to truly believe she is the Blessed Mother—or whatever—and she saved our son?"

Rachel put her hand on his shoulder. "Not just our son, you and our son. Yes, that's what I saw happen and so did thousands of others."

Bob couldn't keep quiet. "Hold on here. You're saying the woman that saved your son is the same one from our radio show? She came on our show to preach to the world—to try and save us?"

"Bob, settle down. There have been sightings of the Blessed Mother all through history. We see unexplained happenings every day, to some they are miracles." Andy looked toward Harry.

"You told me you witnessed two miracles at the school shooting last year."

"Right. I told all of you what I saw and the doctors confirmed it. Without divine intervention, Michael and his son would not be here today. Miracles, Apparitions, Blessed Mother or Goddess—this does not surprise me. This order, group, whatever— they are the good guys. Hell, all Mac and I see everyday is evil. I wish we saw more good, but most days all we see is the devil."

Mac interrupted. "If you don't mind I'd like to say something. I hate to bring this up, but it's stayed with me. I didn't think much of it when it happened…"

"Go on, Mac."

He looked at Michael, then Harry. "You know, Harry, when I called you from the school grounds, we were investigating the disappearance of Michael's sister, Celeste. I told you I had a hunch about where we might find her."

"Yes, you found them digging up the old tennis courts."

"Exactly." Mac exhaled loudly. "Well…damn this sounds crazy. Uh, where to start? I was sitting on the sidelines in the football stadium thinking of Celeste. Then I heard this beautiful whisper. I looked in the direction and saw a young woman with a ponytail. I called to her—no response. So, I followed her. I think she called my name—not really sure; the wind carried it. I almost caught up to her as she turned the corner.

"Next thing I know, I walked right into the path of a bulldozer. It scared the hell out of me. The guy jumped off the dozer to make sure I was all right. I assured him I was, then looked around for the girl. Nowhere to be seen, how did he miss hitting her? The dozer guy looked at me like I was crazy when I asked about her. Then the idea hit me that I could be looking at a crime scene. I called you, Harry, never thought of the girl again—until now."

No one heard Grey walk up. "That's some story."

"Good Lord, Grey, you scared us half to death." Bob wiped his forehead.

"Sorry, I thought you knew I was behind you. Mind if a join you?"

"No, of course, we don't," Rachel responded. "Please, pull up a chair."

Grey motioned to his staff and within minutes they brought wine, coffee, and tea.

"You know, Grey, most everyone here has a story. We haven't heard yours yet. Care to share?"

Grey smiled broadly. "I would love to. I was getting worried no one would ask." He took a sip of coffee before beginning. "My mom and dad took me on a holiday to Greece when I was four. We stayed in a small Greek village outside of Volos. They heard from the villagers that there was a sacred place in a grove of olive trees where people went to pray for favors. Some claimed if you prayed overnight in the grove, your prayer would be answered. And if you were really special, you might see a lovely lady among the trees. Well, my parents had a very specific favor they wanted, so they left me with the nanny and went to pray all night in the grove. My memory of the trip is vague except that I was very sick at the time. They didn't share the whole story with me until I was sixteen. I had been diagnosed with leukemia. Back then, and even now, it was a grim forecast. The whole idea of the trip was to search for a cure. When we got back to the States, I started getting better. The doctors had no explanation. Some said it was a miracle. I only know I have been healthy ever since, except for the occasional cold. What I find so intriguing and why I was captured by the story you told, Mac, my parents said the lady who spoke to them that night had the most captivating voice they had ever heard. Her voice is what they remembered the most."

Father Andy blessed himself. "That's a wonderful story, Grey. Thanks for sharing it with us, but you left out the most important part—what did the lady say?"

"Ah, yes. Sorry to say they never told me, or anyone else."

"Are you serious?"

"I'm afraid so, and believe me I've tried to find out. I think some of the older members like Anca and my folks have been told the same thing, but no one talks about it. Michael, Rachel, did the lady ever speak directly to you?"

"No, not to me. I think she did to my mom. My mom implied it but never really said. You, Michael?"

"No, Rach, just what she said on my show and that was for all to hear." Michael looked at his watch. "Man, it's later than I thought. How about we call it a night? I'm all talked out."

Harry yawned."My sentiments exactly. Thank you for a wonderful evening. I believe you lived up to your word, Grey. This is a night I'll never forget."

They all agreed, said their good-byes, and promised to meet at the Tin Angel for a late brunch.

Michael and Rachel rode home in silence.

THIRTY-THREE

Michael leaned over to kiss Rachel goodnight.

"*Michael, listen... Michael, hear me...*"

"*That voice again? Celeste, is that you?*"

"*Yes, I'm Celeste to you. I am known throughout the world, worshipped or acknowledged in many religions. I am the common thread that binds.*"

Michael sat in the dark. As the room gradually lightened, he realized he was sitting at his desk. He saw Bob and the crew. "*Wait! I thought today was Saturday—meeting friends for lunch. What's going on?*"

"*Michael, hear me. God is slowly disappearing from your world. If you take God out of your life, hope and faith disappear, the children are hopeless—it's easy for evil to invade their minds and souls. Faith is gone. We need to save the children.*"

Bob urged Michael to talk; he was on air. Michael was bewildered. "*I'm losing it. Celeste, what are you talking about?*"

"*Time is short. My love is so great for my children that my Son died to save them—a Child who sacrificed His life so many could live.*"

"*Time is short? I'll give you all the time you want.*"

"*I don't need time, Michael. I have eternity. It's your world that's running out of time. Evil is taking over—eating away the light. Soon it will be covered in a black shroud. Your world needs to accept the truth that there is true evil and the world will end when evil outweighs good...that time is near again.*"

"Michael, you have seen the signs that have been written."

"Michael?"

"Yes, of course I have. When I look at everything that is happening in the world, all the signs are there. I'm immersed in them with this job, but, damn, it's so hard to accept it. I am a man of faith—I should be able to... Why is it so hard to believe? What do you want of me? Not everyone believes in God."

"True, not all believe in the God **you** know, but God is found in many places. For most, even the nonbelievers, their God is remembered only when they face their greatest fear, their darkest hour. Then they cry out for help. Who are they seeking...reaching for... Who?"

"I have no answer."

"That's the problem. You have all forgotten. You have forsaken the Light."

Silence hung between them.

"Please tell me this is a dream."

"Michael, hear me... The time is near. You have been chosen to spread the Word."

"Me? I'm not a prophet."

"True, but you are a champion and protector of the innocents. You have led through His truth."

"I have fallen short."

"No, Michael. Because of your devotion to children, you have found favor with your God."

"I am humbled. What do you want me to do?"

"Keep faith and hope in your heart, Michael. Ask your listeners around the world this question: Who...who do they seek?"

"That's it?"

"No, Michael. Pray for the right answer."

"Celeste, Celeste... CELESTE!"

About the Authors

Animals, art and reading have been a part of **CC Smith's** life since she was a young child. Having horses in Pennsylvania, raising a lion cub in Philly, owning a tea room and art gallery in Texas have all been dreams come true.

She is an avid gardener and received several awards for gardens she created in St. Louis. While in St. Louis, she was the campaign manager for a state representative, president of a neighborhood association and authored the newsletter.

CC helped to gain historic registration for her district, worked to build two city dog parks and was involved in raising money for a new animal shelter.

She loves painting and photography, but writing has always been her passion. Her first short story appeared in the award winning L&L Dreamspell anthology, *A Box of Texas Chocolates*.

Now, back in Texas and living in Galveston—another dream has been realized.

Betty Gordon connected with words and symbols at a young age. On Sunday visits to her grandparents, she investigated their book shelves, pulled out chemistry books, and stared at formulas she couldn't understand. Even so, the formulas held magic that materialized into writing poetry, non-fiction, and fiction.

Betty is the author of *Murder in the Third Person, Deceptive Clarity*, and *The Magic of Christmas*, a collection of short stories. Her novel, *Valley of Obsessions*, was released in 2011. She has also published numerous works in L&L Dreamspell's anthologies, *Dead and Breakfast*, award winning *A Death in Texas, A Box of Texas Chocolates*, and *Twisted Tales of Texas Landmarks*.

She enjoys membership in Mystery Writers of America, Sisters in Crime, Writers' League of Texas, Houston Writers Guild, The Final Twist, and Bay Area Writers' League.

CPSIA information can be obtained at www.ICGtesting.com
Printed in the USA
237239LV00001B/7/P

9 781603 183109